THE RENEGADES

The hangman's noose was waiting for Bart Foraker unless he could reach the safety of the Mexican border. Wanted for a crime he didn't commit, Bart swore he'd come back to clear his name. Right now, escape was the only thing on his mind. Then he found Meg Swope, sole survivor of a bloody Indian massacre. Bart galloped back into danger—with a lynch-crazy posse hot on his tail, and a price on his head that set every bounty hunter's gun against him . . .

THE RENEGADES

Ray Hogan

GUNSMOKE

This hardback edition 2006
by BBC Audiobooks Ltd
by arrangement with
Golden West Literary Agency

ISBN 10: 1 4056 8089 X
ISBN 13: 978 1 405 68089 9

British Library Cataloguing in Publication Data available.

Printed and bound in Great Britain by
Antony Rowe Ltd., Chippenham, Wiltshire

★ 1 ★

"If I had my choosings," Deputy Pete Worley said, giving Foraker a hard shove and sending him stumbling into Red Bluff's makeshift jail, "you'd be swinging from a tree limb right now."

Foraker caught his balance and, anger pouring through him, spun to face Worley, a young, sly-faced man who had harassed him constantly since the posse had picked him up in his camp along Foreman's Creek.

"Yeh, I reckon you would," he snarled, "and I'm wondering why you're so damned anxious. Maybe you know more about that rancher's wife than you're letting on."

"Was you that killed her after you got done having yourself a time with her," Worley snapped.

Foraker shrugged wearily. A young man in his early twenties, he was a muscular six feet; sun-browned to the extreme, he had dark hair, cool, blue eyes, a neglected mustache, and a ragged stubble of beard. Dressed in faded denim pants, gray shield shirt, scuffed, flat-heeled boots, red bandanna, and low-crowned brown hat, he looked to be any drifter riding through a frontier town.

"I had nothing to do with that," he said doggedly. "Told you, and the sheriff, that a half a dozen times, but nobody's willing to listen."

"Sure, sure, you ain't guilty—same as me," a voice coming from a dark corner of the old store building

1

commented dryly. "Wouldn't nobody listen to me either, pardner."

Bart Foraker turned to face the speaker as Worley jerked the door shut and united a hasp and padlock on its outer side.

"Name's Crockett. Friends call me Reno," the voice continued, and then materialized into a husky, thick-shouldered redheaded man with a warped smile.

Thumbs hooked into the pockets of his vest, wearing the remains of a once-blue suit, he stepped into the fading daylight slanting down from a hole in the tin roof of the old building.

"They got me in here waiting for a U.S. marshal to take me to Trinidad—that's down Colorado way—where they aim to string me up for murder, too. Wasn't me that done it either," he added with a laugh.

Foraker considered the squat, sandy-looking man thoughtfully—and took an instant dislike to him. Crockett had a snide, surly way that rankled Bart and intensified the soaring frustration that filled him.

"Can do all the laughing and funning you want," he said coldly, "but I ain't guilty of raping and killing that woman—and I sure don't aim to let no judge hang me for it."

Crockett gave that thought. Then, "I reckon that means you're figuring on jumping this two-bit chicken coop before the judge gets here."

Foraker made no reply, simply pivoted on a heel and began to circle the single, dirt-floored room, staying close to its rock walls as he searched for a suggestion that would permit an escape.

"Hell, you're wasting your time," Reno said in disgust after a few minutes. "You ain't about to bust a hole in them walls."

"Can see that," Foraker muttered, continuing his investigation.

The circuit almost completed, he halted, glanced up. The building had no ceiling, just a corrugated tin roof which had rusted through in several places.

"You ain't getting out that way either," Crockett stated in his irritating manner. "Take a man twenty feet tall to get up there, and then there ain't none of them holes big enough for him to squeeze through."

"How long have you been in here?" Foraker asked, bringing his attention back to Crockett.

"Five days, counting this one."

"And you ain't tried getting out?"

Reno shrugged his thick shoulders. "Thought about it and done some looking around, same as you. Figured there ain't no way it could be done."

Bart shook his head. "There's got to be—we haven't found it yet. Who feeds us?"

"A woman that runs a boardinghouse up the street a piece. Brings in a plate of whatever she's serving that day for supper—usually salt pork and beans, or maybe it'll be potatoes or some greens. Biscuits are good, howsomever, but the chicory she brews up'll take the hair off a buffalo."

"Who comes with her?"

"The deputy—Worley—most times. The sheriff, old man Burke, has come once or twice."

"What time?"

Crockett's features had become quiet, his small, brown eyes intent. "Mornings it's not long after sunup. Supper gets here late—maybe seven or eight o'clock. I expect the woman waits until all the regular paying customers are done eating, then brings us the leftovers."

"Worley come inside with her?"

Reno folded his arms, stepped up closer to Foraker. "You thinking what I figure you're thinking—jump Worley when the woman shows up with our grub?"

Foraker turned, studied the door through which he

3

had just entered. It was not in any way offset, but was flush with the thick rock wall in which it had been hung. There was, however, a space of two feet or so on its north side where the two walls met to create a corner. A man could stand there in the dark, and be unseen.

"You getting yourself an idea?" Reno asked, squatting on his heels. "Well, mister, you sure better count me in, else I'll holler and sure'n hell spoil it for you."

Bart mulled that about in his mind. The chances of successfully pulling off an escape alone were fair if done along the lines he was planning; with the help of Crockett they would be considerably better.

"Not sure you've got the guts," Foraker said flatly, "else you would have tried your hand before."

Reno Crockett bristled, came to his feet. "Ain't nobody ever said something like that to me before—and lived to brag about it! You just tell me what you want me to do, and I'll sure'n hell do it!"

Foraker came back around, studied the outlaw. Light inside the jail was growing dim. It would not be long until sundown—and then would come the moment when the woman would arrive with the evening meal, and the time would be at hand to make his move—now with Reno Crockett as a partner, it would seem. Maybe it would work, and there was a chance it would fail; he would end up dead, shot down by Pete Worley, who had gone out of his way to make things tough for him, or by Eben Burke, the county's elderly sheriff. But better that than going up before a judge, due to arrive that next day, and being sentenced to the gallows—which certainly would be his fate as every member of the posse, and both lawmen, would swear to his guilt.

"All right," Foraker said, "you're with me. I'll tell you what I'm aiming to do later—but it'll be when they

4

bring us supper. Your horse in that livery stable at the end of the street?"

"Was, last I seen of him—"

"That's where they put my bay. Once we're out of here we'll have to get to that stable fast without anybody seeing us, grab our horses, and make tracks."

"Which way will we be going?"

"I'm figuring to head south into Kansas, across the Oklahoma panhandle into New Mexico. Once I make it to there I'll be in country where I know the back trails like I know the back of my hand. Got plenty of friends along there, too, who'll let me hole up if a posse starts nipping at my heels."

"You going to just stay in New Mexico?"

"No—be passing through. Best place for any man with the law after him is Mexico."

Crockett rubbed at his jaw. "Well, hearing you say you know all about the country down there—which I sure don't—why, I reckon I'll just string along with you. Mexico sure sounds like a good idea, too."

Foraker frowned. He hadn't planned on a traveling companion. "Where'd you go if I wasn't around and you got out of here?"

"Never give it no thought," the outlaw replied. "Most likely toward Dodge City, but any direction would be all right. One's just as good as another—I just ain't much acquainted nowhere around here."

Foraker nodded, moved over to the nearby wall, and squatting, rested against it. The day had been a long, hard one and he was dead tired—most of his weariness stemming from being rousted about by Deputy Pete Worley and some of the posse members during the half-day ride back from his camp to Red Bluff. He'd not be at his best to make an escape attempt, but with the judge before whom he would stand trial for murder due within only hours, he had no alternative.

"This here scheme you've got cooked up, you for damn sure it'll work?"

At Crockett's question Bart shrugged. "There ain't nothing for sure but death and the sun coming up and going down! Maybe it'll work, and maybe it won't, but with what I'm faced I've got no choice except to make a try. If you're wanting to back out, you're welcome to do it. Going along will suit me a lot better."

"Nope—now just hold on! I ain't backing out," Reno said quickly. "Mexico's where I want to go, and since I don't know nothing about getting there, and you do, I'm smart enough to stick close to you. . . . Now, you want to tell me how we're pulling off this here miracle?"

Foraker glanced up at the holes in the roof of the old building. Stars were visible in the sky; night had set in.

"Yeh, expect we'd better get ready—they'll be coming with supper soon," he said. "This here's what I figure to do."

★ **2** ★

A short time later, tension building steadily within him, Bart Foraker pulled back deeper into the corner adjacent to the door. The sound of approaching footsteps had suddenly become definite, and it would be only moments until he knew if his efforts to escape would succeed or not. ...

Should there be failure it would not be because his planning was faulty; he had placed Reno Crockett in the far side of the room where a pile of straw served as a bed, and by using his own shirt and hat, he created a figure that from the doorway resembled a body. Reno, as desperate now as he to escape, knew exactly what he was to do.

The padlock chinked against the hasp. Pete Worley said something unintelligible, and the woman with him laughed. Bart tensed as the door opened.

"Over here, Deputy," Crockett called. "Been trying to get word to you—this jasper you throwed in here with me's gone and cut his own throat!"

A curse ripped from Worley's lips. The woman, carrying a tray, stepped through the entrance and was pushed roughly aside by the deputy as he crowded hurriedly past her.

In that moment, hands locked together forming a club, Foraker glided out of the dark corner where he was crouched, in behind the lawman, and swinging with all his strength, drove a shocking blow into the side of Worley's head. The woman screamed and dropped the tray of food she was holding as the deputy went sprawling onto the dirt floor.

"Shut up!" Foraker snapped at the woman, and snatching up the lawman's pistol, he wheeled to the door and kicked it shut.

Crockett, prepared for the moment, had crossed to where Pete Worley lay and was removing the man's gun belt. Hanging on to it for several moments, he tossed it to Foraker and wheeled to the woman.

"You want to keep on living?" he demanded roughly.

She managed a sobbing reply in the affirmative.

"Then you set right there where you are and keep your mouth shut till somebody comes along and lets you and the deputy out. Hear?"

"You—you ain't going to—to kill me?"

"Not if you're quiet like Reno said," Foraker replied, buckling on the deputy's gun belt and pistol and retrieving his hat and shirt.

Time was passing swiftly, and knowing they had none to spare, Bart moved swiftly. Moving to the door, he opened it slightly and cautiously glanced out. There was no one to be seen on the darkened street, the only signs of life appearing to be at the town's two saloons, where both noise and light were in evidence.

"Let's go," he said in a hoarse whisper to Crockett.

Reno was immediately at his side and followed him into the open. "Been thinking maybe we ought've buffaloed them two good, made for damn sure they'd stay quiet."

The woman began to sob anxiously again. Foraker shook his head. "No need. Doubt if anybody'll be coming around for a few minutes," he said, and pulling the door closed, set the hasp and padlock. "Let's get to the

8

horses," he continued, and pivoting, hurried off into the night for the livery barn at the end of the street.

Panting to keep up, Crockett said, "Still figure it'd been smart to cold-cock them two. I owe that damned deputy a few—"

"Same here," Foraker cut in, "but we couldn't afford the time. I expect we've got maybe thirty minutes before somebody misses the woman and comes looking for her—and then it'll be maybe another thirty minutes until Eben Burke gets a posse together and starts hunting us. Which means we've got an hour or less to get the horses and light out—and get as far from here as possible."

"There's the stable . . ."

Foraker slowed to a fast walk, still keeping well within the shadows lying along the side of the dusty street.

"Lamp burning in there somewhere," Crockett said.

"Hostler most likely. Was hoping we'd not find anybody here, it being night."

"We going right in through the door?" Reno asked, halting at the edge of the wide opening in the front of the sprawling, low-roofed structure.

Foraker nodded. "We don't have time to hunt up some other way. We'll try slipping in, going down the runway without making any racket. I'll take care of the hostler, or whoever is in there—you be finding the horses. Mine's a bay with black stockings and a blaze face."

Crockett murmured his understanding and fell silent as they entered the barn. Drawing the pistol taken from Pete Worley, Bart Foraker, followed by the outlaw, eased along the wall and silently made his way toward the open doorway, from which light was coming. Farther on in the stable another lantern, turned low, could now be seen.

9

Coming to a stop at the doorway of what apparently was the office, Foraker glanced carefully inside. A man was sitting in a chair reading a magazine. Bart turned to Crockett, motioned for him to continue on in search of the horses. At once Reno moved by, but not without first muttering his displeasure at something. As he crossed in front of the open doorway, motion caught the hostler's eye.

"Hey," he yelled, laying aside the yellowing magazine and coming to his feet. "What're you wanting?"

Coming about, he crossed the office and stepped out into the runway.

"Just getting our horses," Foraker replied softly from the shadows, and rapped the man sharply across the temple with his pistol.

He caught the hostler as he crumpled, and dragging him back into the office, tied him to the chair in which he had been sitting. He could find nothing with which to gag the man, and abandoning a brief search, returned to the runway and hurried to join Crockett.

"Find them?" he asked, seeing the outlaw at the corral outside the stable's rear doors.

"Looks like your animal over there," Reno replied. "Still saddled and bridled. Can't spot mine. He's a kind of a gray—"

"Better grab whatever's handy—we haven't got time to waste in hunting him," Bart said, and hurried to the bay.

A stir of anger passed through him when he reached the big gelding. The horse was just as he was when he'd dismounted from him several hours earlier—cinch still tight, bit yet between his teeth. The hostler, uncaring and lazy, likely intended to let the animal stand around until the following day before removing the gear and feeding and watering him. But Bart guessed there was a

10

good side to it; it wouldn't be necessary to spend time saddling and bridling him.

Freeing the reins, which were looped about the corral's top bar, Foraker paused to listen for any sounds that might be coming from the street, and hearing none, he swung up onto the bay and came about. Crockett had chosen a tall black mount, was in the act of pulling tight the cinch and mounting.

"You get me a gun?" he asked, settling into the hull.

"Nope—never thought. Don't think the hostler was wearing one, but like as not there'll be one in the office. Can look in a drawer of the desk I saw up against a wall—"

Reno cursed angrily, and riding across the corral, opened the gate. "Dammit, you should've thought to get me one while you was in there," he said, and turning into the barn, rode hurriedly up the runway to the stable's office.

Foraker followed the outlaw into the open, but did not reenter the building, waiting instead in the darkness behind it. He saw Crockett dismount when he reached the office, disappear inside, and then shortly reappear. Vaulting back onto the black, the outlaw retraced his course along the runway and outside the barn to where Foraker waited.

"Had to give that hostler another rap on the head," he said. "Was coming to—I reckon you didn't do a good-enough job on him. And there's a commotion of some kind going on down the street. Expect somebody's found the deputy and the woman."

"Likely," Foraker said, swinging the bay about and moving off into the night, now beginning to cloud up. "You get yourself a gun?"

"Sure did," Crockett replied, moving in beside him. "Ain't much—an old army cap and ball that's been

11

fixed. Got a handful of cartridges, too, but there wasn't no holster. Which way you figure we best head out?"

"West—"

"West?" Crockett echoed. "What the hell're we going that direction for? Ought to go south!"

"Aim to, after a bit. I recollect there's some brushy hills west of here. We reach them we'll have cover in case a posse picks up our trail in a hurry. Can swing south once we're in the clear."

Reno shrugged a reluctant agreement and then added, "Sure ain't much of a horse I got—and the damn saddle feels like the cantle's busted. Ought've took time to find my own animal and gear."

"Time was something we didn't have much of," Bart said, patience growing thin. "Said yourself there was some kind of a ruckus going on in the street. Most likely it was at the jail. Either they'd got the deputy and the woman out, or were busting down the door."

"About it. Should've took care of them two like I wanted," Reno grumbled as they pressed steadily on.

Most of the stars overhead had disappeared behind clouds, which was making for poor visibility, but such created no great problem; the plain across which they were riding was mostly level, with only an occasional gully to break its evenness, leaving only the danger of the horses stepping into a gopher or prairie-dog hole.

Luck, however, was with them. They reached the low, bubblelike hills Foraker had in mind without mishap, and quickly disappeared into the brush that grew thick along their slopes and in the washes lying between.

They would go as far as they could before daylight, Bart decided, and then it would be not only smart but necessary to halt. His horse, having been in use most of that day, would need to rest; and such could be true of the black Crockett was riding, since it probably belonged to one of the posse members.

12

Too, Foraker wanted to see if Sheriff Burke had made up a posse and was on their trail; whatever the answer to that question was would determine the course he and Reno would take.

★ 3 ★

The early sun, flooding the flats and hills with molten gold, found Bart Foraker and Reno Crockett camped on the crest of a fairly high wooded rise. They had not covered as much ground as Foraker had hoped, due to the condition of both horses, and they had pulled to a stop much sooner than he had expected. Still he reckoned they had done right well, considering, and probably had put at least twenty miles between them and Red Bluff.

"You got something to eat in them saddlebags?" Reno asked in a peevish voice. He was squatted close by while Foraker stared out across the brightening land searching for riders.

"Nope," Bart replied. "Had a grub sack hanging on my saddle when that posse grabbed me. One of them must have took it."

"Oh, hell!" Crockett muttered in disgust. "We're in one devil of a shape—caught out here in the brakes, hungry, flat broke, and a posse on our tails—"

"And in country where renegade Apaches are said to be running loose everywhere," Foraker cut in dryly.

"Apaches," Crockett repeated in a falling voice, and spat. "That's all we need right now. Damn it all, I should've stayed put there in that jail, took my chances on getting away from that marshal that was coming after me."

"You can always give yourself up when the posse

14

comes along," Foraker said, turning back to the horses. "Ain't more'n a few miles north of us."

Crockett came to his feet hastily and threw his glance into the direction Bart had mentioned. Again he swore.

"Hell—there's at least a dozen in the bunch! You think they've found our tracks?"

"More'n likely. Working this direction."

"How far are we from the Kansas border?"

"Twenty, maybe twenty-five miles."

"Then let's be getting there! Once we cross over, that damned sheriff'll have to pull in his horns. What about a town—there one anywheres close?"

"One on Beaver Creek, I recollect. Just about on the state line."

"Well, just you get me to it and I'll rustle us up some grub—enough to last us for a spell. That's my line of work: busting into some store."

"Stealing—that what you mean?"

"That's just what I'm talking about. What the hell's wrong with that? We're both dead broke, thanks to that lousy sheriff who cleaned my pockets—and yours, too, I expect."

Foraker nodded.

"So we'll do the only thing we can—help ourselves to some counter-jumper's stock of groceries first chance we get, unless you can come up with a better idea."

Foraker said, "Nope, sure can't. Reckon we could shoot us a rabbit or two, or maybe come across an antelope—"

"How about a couple of fat prairie dogs?" Crockett broke in sarcastically. "Not for me, mister! If you think I'm going to be living on varmints all the way to Mexico, then you've got the wrong bull by the tail! I'm scaring us up a grub sack full of regular eating, and if you don't like the how of the way I do it, why, you just better look the other direction!"

"I'm not objecting," Foraker said with a shrug, "I just don't like doing it that way."

Crockett nodded, spat, tugged at the collar of his shirt. "Good. Now maybe if it's chawing at your conscience, and you're big and rich and got a pocketful of money, you can drop back by and pay the counter-jumper for what I took. Only you best not explain what you're doing; if he's like most of his kind I've come across, the son of a bitch'll call the law and have you thrown into jail just for the hell of it."

Foraker laughed as he tightened the bay's cinch. "Could be. . . . You come from a cussing family?"

Reno grinned as he prepared to mount. "No—was just the other way around. Didn't have no pa, so it was Ma who run the farm and raised us kids. Every time me or one of my brothers said a bad word, as she called them, she slapped our jaws good. Day she cashed in, I went around saying every cuss word I could think of. Guess doing it sort of stuck with me." The outlaw paused, studied Bart closely. "Why? It bother you?"

"Nope, not especially. Always figured swearing was a sort of habit a man can get in, like sleeping with his boots on. You ready to move out?"

"Anytime," the outlaw said, and swung up into his saddle.

Foraker mounted also and headed the bay down the back side of the rise, thus keeping the formation with its growth of brush and squat trees between them and the distant posse.

"Best we take it slow and easy," he said. "Got to keep our eyes peeled for Indians."

"Yeh, along with that damned posse—"

Foraker agreed. "We know where Burke is, though, and all we have to do is keep off high ground and not give them a chance to see us. It's the Apaches we can't be sure of."

16

They rode on, following a circuitous route that kept them not only below the horizon but within the brushy areas as well. Several times at strategic points Foraker would cut away and carefully survey the surrounding country for signs of danger, but he found nothing to cause alarm; if there were Apache marauders prowling the hills and flats, they were not in evidence—and the posse from Red Bluff was no longer in sight.

"You reckon that sheriff has called off hunting us?" Crockett wondered hopefully.

"Not likely—especially if he's got a U.S. marshal with him."

"Expect you're right. They've got plenty of big reasons for wanting us both—real bad." Crockett paused and, grasping the horn, twisted half about to relieve the discomfort of his ill-fitting saddle.

"That for true you claiming you didn't kill that rancher's wife?"

"For true," Bart said. "Got me a hunch who did it, but the sheriff wouldn't give me a chance to try and prove it. . . . Something I aim to do once I get on the yonder side of the Mexican border and can let things simmer down. Figure to come back, straighten it all out. You in the same fix?"

Crockett shook his head, tipped his hat forward to shield his eyes from the sun. "Nope, can't do nothing but own up to what they say I done. Was a half dozen jaybirds seen me do it—seen me gun down a fellow. Wasn't the first one, either, so I reckon I can't holler much if they catch me again. Ain't that smoke on ahead a few miles?"

"I've been watching it, trying to decide if it's a low cloud or not, but I reckon it's smoke, sure enough." He glanced up at the slowly clearing sky. "Can't be sure—us swinging wide like we did—but it could be Danburg, the town I was telling you about."

17

Reno jerked off his high-crowned, Texas-style hat and brushed at the sweat beading his forehead. "Those are sure sweet-sounding words—'cause I'm hungry enough to eat a polecat, tail and all! Looks like we ought to get there about dark."

"About—"

"First off, we'll find us a store where there'll be grub and wait till it's closed. Then I'll go in and help myself."

Foraker grinned at Reno Crockett's offhand manner. "Let's keep hoping it'll be that easy."

"Can bet on it—just you leave it to me," Reno said confidently.

And Crockett was right—or partly so. They reached Danburg well after dark, found everything closed up but the town's one saloon. The general store stood off by itself, well back from the street near the center of the settlement, and leaving Bart to wait with the horses in a patch of brush at the rear of the building, Reno skillfully raised a window, entered, and returned a half-hour or less later with a sugar sack containing not only an ample supply of trail grub, but the necessary utensils to prepare and eat the food.

A hard grin cracked his mouth as he mounted. "We sure better not hang around here, pardner," he said. "Jasper owning that store lives in the back, and I got him to stirring around when I knocked over a stack of water buckets. How far are we from Kansas?"

"Four miles or so," Foraker replied, eyes on a rear window in the store building that had suddenly filled with light. "Expect we better be getting there fast."

Crockett again grinned at Bart. Even through the pale starlight the excitement dancing in the outlaw's eyes was apparent.

"Lead the way, pardner—I'll be right behind you," he said.

18

They pressed on steadily for a good hour, and when they were well into Kansas, pulled up alongside small willow-bound creek and made camp.

"You doing the cooking?" Crockett asked. "Seems I done the getting, reckon you ought to do the fixing."

Foraker's shoulders stirred indifferently. It didn't matter one way or another to him; he'd put together a thousand or more meals on the trail in the past, and one more, or a dozen, was neither here nor there. Too, he was in no mood to argue the point with the outlaw; he had long since regretted he had agreed to take the man with him to Mexico.

Grabbing the sugar sack, he squatted down near a likely place for a fire and began to lay out the food and utensils for a meal. Crockett, a few strides away, had settled down, his back to a tree, and was lighting one of the black stogies he had apparently obtained during the robbery of the store in Danburg. Bart shrugged impatiently.

"Can use some wood for the fire—and you best look to the horses. Need to unsaddle them, and—"

"There ain't no hurry," Crockett said with a wave of his hand. "And I reckon I don't need nobody telling me what—"

"Suit yourself," Foraker cut in, rising. "I aim to see to my horse because I'll be needing him tomorrow—and the next few days after that. You'll have to wait on eating till I've taken care of him and rustled up some firewood."

"Oh, hell," Crockett shouted, coming to his feet. "I'll rustle you up some firewood, so keep at your cooking—I'm plain starved. And I'll look after the damn horses."

Foraker resumed his chore, scooping out a shallow dip in the soil and arranging rocks around it to form a fire pit. Crockett returned with an armload of dry branches, dropped the fuel nearby, and strode off to take care of the horses. Raking some of the branches into the pit, Bart started a fire, and filling the coffeepot from the creek, set it over the flames. That done, he then filled the frying pan with chunks of salt pork, potatoes, onions, and a can of beans. Adding a small amount of water, he placed the spider over the fire also.

The wood Reno had brought would not last for long, and Foraker now set about collecting more, forgoing the thought of reminding Reno Crockett of the need. This time he would handle it himself—for the sake of the weary, all-important horses, for should either of them break down somewhere in the long desolate miles that lay ahead of them, they would be in serious, if not fatal trouble. As he had mentioned to Crockett, there was little if any possibility that Eben Burke would call off his posse.

The posse . . . Foraker dropped to his haunches beside the fire, added a handful of the powder-dry sticks to it, and after tearing off two chunks from the loaf of bread he found in the sack and placing them on the rocks encircling the fire to warm, he rose and climbed a nearby mound for a look to the north.

A faint red spot in the night, well in the distance, marked a campfire. The posse—there was little doubt of it. Indians would have sought out a hidden place—down in a deep wash or in a thick stand of brush and trees, as had he. Eben Burke apparently didn't trouble to hide his presence, being convinced that sooner or later he would run his escaped prisoners to ground. Pivoting, Bart returned to the camp.

"Where the hell you been?" Crockett demanded as Foraker resumed his place by the fire. "Stuff in the frying pan's about to boil over, and there ain't no coffee beans been mashed and put in the pot."

"Go ahead, mash up a handful, dump it in the water," Bart said indifferently.

20

Crockett mumbled a curse, squatted, and searching about in the grub sack, found the package of coffee. Opening it, he swore again.

"Hell, it's done been ground," he muttered, and added a quantity to the water gurgling in the blackening pot. "Was you out there looking for the posse?"

Foraker nodded, took up a stick, and began to stir the concoction in the frying pan.

"Can see their fire—pretty far north of us."

Crockett's brow knitted into a concerned frown. "Means we best ride out soon's we eat."

Bart shook his head, paused to listen to the distant wailing of a coyote. "No, be smart to let the horses rest. There's plenty of grass and water—"

"Dammit!" the outlaw exploded. "Where do you get off calling all the shots! Hell, I know as much about things like this as you—and I say we best move on."

"No need," Foraker said quietly, continuing to stir. "Their horses are needing rest same as ours. The sheriff won't move out till sunup."

"That's what you're thinking. You could be wrong, mister, and I ain't for taking no chances."

"Suit yourself," Bart said, reaching for one of the tin plates. Crockett had thought of about everything, it seemed, except something to eat with. "Head out on your own whenever you're ready, Mexico's due south and a couple of weeks away."

The outlaw muttered under his breath, took up a plate, and extended it toward Foraker. "I'll do some thinking about it. . . . If that stew's fit to eat, dish me out some."

No more was said about the possibility of Reno Crockett striking out by himself, and they spent the night by the creek. Both men were up early, and after a quick breakfast of fried salt pork, warmed-over bread,

21

and reheated black coffee left over from the night before, they again went into the saddles and moved south.

From then on and in the days that followed, a game of hound and hares developed with Foraker and Crockett enacting the role of the latter while Eben Burke and his posse played the relentless pursuers.

They crossed Kansas, entered the outlaw haven country of the Oklahoma panhandle commonly known as No-Man's-Land, and moved into New Mexico Territory. Several times in the past they had caught sight of the posse doggedly trailing them in the far distance, and try as he would, Foraker could in no way dislodge the lawman and his party from their trail. It eventually dawned on Bart that Burke was employing an expert tracker and that shaking the posse was going to be most difficult.

But strangely enough, after a day in the New Mexico hill country, where there was considerable cover in the way of brush, trees, and deep arroyos, they lost sight of the posse.

"Hell—we've done gone and ditched them!" Crockett declared joyously. "They ain't nowheres in sight. They're gone!"

"Could be," Foraker agreed, but only halfheartedly. Had it been in the cards to shake Burke, he felt it would have occurred back in the Oklahoma panhandle, where there were countless trails going in all directions. It wasn't logical they would give the posse the slip right after entering New Mexico.

But they saw nothing of Eben Burke and his men—not that first day or during the succeeding four, and finally Bart Foraker, too, began to believe they were at last free of the stubbornly pursuing lawmen from Red Bluff.

"Smoke over there by them bluffs," Crockett said around midafternoon as they rode steadily south. "You

22

reckon it's a town, or maybe a ranch? I could sure use a good, square meal."

Bart Foraker had been studying the distant dark smudge in the otherwise unstained blue of the sky for some time. Familiar with the area, he could recall neither a settlement nor a rancher being there.

"Not that I recollect," he said, answering the outlaw's hope-filled question. "Road comes in there from the east—sort of a shortcut out of Texas, and that's all. Maybe we best take a look."

An hour later they approached the lazily spiraling column of smoke which was rising from the depths of a large arroyo beyond which a band of dense brush meandered off into the flats.

"Could be Indians—Apaches or maybe Comanches," Bart said as they drew to a halt beside a juniper. "Best we go careful."

"For damn sure," Crockett said as they dismounted and started forward slowly on foot. "It sure is quiet."

Approaching the edge of the large wash, both men dropped lower and, hats off, crawled the last few yards. Reaching the rim, they halted abruptly. An oath blurted from Crockett's lips. Bart Foraker shook his head.

It was the remains of a three-wagon immigrant party. Indians had struck without warning, apparently, catching the men off guard. A half a dozen or more bodies were visible and lay strewn about among the still-smoldering vehicles and the scattered household items and personal possessions left unwanted by the marauding savages.

★ 4 ★

"Ain't nobody down there that's alive," Crockett said, starting to rise.

Foraker pulled the outlaw back down. "Maybe, but best we be certain. And we need to go careful. The Indians could still be hanging around."

"Let them hang," Reno said. "Ain't no call for us to go poking around in a massacre."

Bart, still prone, drew himself back a short distance from the arroyo, and then got to his feet.

"Those folks need burying—can't just leave them laying out there for the buzzards and varmints to get at."

Crockett, now also upright, shrugged. "Why not? It won't bother them none 'cause they won't know nothing about it. Besides, we ain't got the time to spare—you keep telling me that, and we don't know for sure where that posse is."

Foraker turned to his horse and went into the saddle. Giving the brush beyond the arroyo a careful probing, he swiped at the sweat on his face.

"Can do what you please, Reno. I'm having me a look over there on the other side of the wash to be sure the Apaches, or whatever they were, are gone—then I'm going to take care of those people."

Raking the bay lightly with his spurs, Bart cut the big horse about and began a wide circle that would bring

24

him into the brakes area beyond the arroyo with its death and burned remnants of a wagon train.

He did not look back to see if Crockett was following or if he had elected to continue southward on his own; indeed, he did not care. The outlaw had proved to be even more disagreeable and perverse than he had earlier thought. But when Bart finally reached the heavy brush east of the arroyo, he found Crockett only a stride or two behind him, patiently and carefully moving in and out of the rank growth in search of any sign of the renegade Indians.

They found where the braves had waited in ambush for the immigrants to reach the arroyo and start to cross, noting also that the Indians apparently returned to the same spot when the attack was over, for there were spots of blood on the leaves of several bushes—either from a wounded brave or from a horse.

"I reckon they've gone on," Crockett said, "so let's start the burying—if you're still set on doing it."

Foraker only nodded and rode out of the screening brush and down into the sandy arroyo. The bay was skittish from the smell of death and the acrid smoke, and dismounting a short distance from the grisly scene, Bart tied the animal to a stout piñon tree. Crockett followed his example, and then both men dropped back to the site of the attack.

"You ain't figuring on digging graves for all of them, are you?" the outlaw asked, again protesting.

Eight bodies all told: three women, four men—stripped and badly mutilated. There was also one Indian—an Apache, Bart saw. Little was left of the pilgrims' possessions, the Indians having claimed everything that was of value to them; what was of no interest they tossed into the burning wagons. The horses, harness and all, were of course gone, the leather straps being prized almost as highly as the animals.

25

"There ain't nothing we can dig with," Crockett grumbled. "Damned redskins done burned up everything."

"We'll have to carry the bodies over to that ravine coming in from the brakes," Foraker said at last. The brutal murders of the immigrants had shocked and unnerved him, but he was determined to see they got as decent a burial as possible. "Can cave in the sides of the gully to cover them over. Then we can carry in some rocks, pile them on top to keep the coyotes from digging them up."

Reno nodded, evidently pleased to hear the chore with which they were faced would be much easier than he'd anticipated.

"What about the redskin?" he asked. "Why don't we just throw him into the fire?"

Foraker was already moving toward the nearest of the bodies, glancing as he did at the vultures circling overhead.

"Can put him in the ravine, too—but not with the others." Foraker paused, bent down and picked up the blade from a broken knife, and thrust it into his pocket. It would come in handy opening cans—replace the sharp stone he'd been forced, from necessity, to use. "Can't savvy him being here. Indians don't usually leave their dead, but generally tote them back to camp."

"I reckon this'n just didn't have no friends," Reno said dryly, and grasping the Apache by one of his outflung arms, dragged him over to the small gully.

What was more likely, Foraker guessed, was that the party of braves had broken off from the main tribe, become outlaws, and were acting on their own.

Moving on to the nearest immigrant—dead from an arrow in the chest and a blow from a tomahawk that had split his skull—Bart hesitated again, his eyes catching sight of a square of canvas not yet completely

26

consumed by fire. Stepping in close to the tarp, he pulled it clear of the overturned, charred wagon, tramped out the edge that was still smoldering. That done, he carried it to the ravine and stretched it out in the cleft's widest place.

"We'll lay the bodies on that," he explained as Reno paused to watch.

The outlaw shrugged. "I'm saying again—ain't nothing going to make any difference to those folks," he declared, and continuing on, took up the ravaged remains of a woman and carried it to the tarp.

Bart had removed that of the man he had first approached, and then together, working systematically but constantly on the alert for any sign of the Indians returning—or of Eben Burke's posse—they placed the unfortunate pilgrims on the canvas, folded it over to cover them, and then broke down the ragged walls of the ravine onto the shrouded figures.

There wasn't sufficient dirt to make a satisfactory grave, and Foraker began to carry in rocks to complete the interment. Crockett offered no help in this, but occupied himself with kicking dirt over the Apache's body, laid a few strides above the point where the settlers had been placed. When they were finished, he pulled off his hat, brushed at the sweat on his face, and glared at Foraker.

"It all right if we go on now?"

The outlaw's tone rankled Bart Foraker, but he held on to his temper, merely glanced skyward again at the circling vultures. There were a dozen or more of the big broad-winged birds wheeling silently against a background of blue now, but they would find nothing to satisfy them when they dropped down to investigate the destruction below.

"I reckon so," he said in reply to Crockett, and coming about, started for the horses.

Bart Foraker came to an abrupt halt. Standing at the edge of the brush was a disheveled, frightened-looking girl. Somewhere in her mid-teens, she was staring at them in a numb, mindless kind of way.

★ 5 ★

"God in heaven!" Foraker blurted, giving a quick thought to what the girl had been through. "How did she—"

"Thing is," Crockett observed, "she's alive. What the hell are we going—"

Foraker brushed the outlaw's question aside before it was completed and, mustering a reassuring smile, started toward the girl. Instantly her features tightened and her eyes spread with alarm.

"Wait—don't be scared of us," he called. "We want to help you."

Suddenly, when Bart was little more than an arm's length from her, the girl whirled and bolted into the brush. Foraker reacted instantly; he would have to catch her—they couldn't leave her there helpless and alone.

The girl darted in and out of the brush like a frightened rabbit, dodging from side to side as fear drove her wildly on. Bart, sweating, breathing hard from running, did not let up on the pursuit. And then, abruptly, it was over. The girl, in frantic flight, turned to throw a glance at Bart Foraker. She failed to see a small juniper directly in her path, plunged into it, and was thrown back and to the ground. Foraker was upon her at once, big hands pressing her slim shoulders firmly down.

"You're all right," he managed between gasps for breath. "I—we won't hurt you."

29

She stared up at him through widespread eyes, the pale gray-blue heightened by the terror that gripped her. Dirt smudged her face, and bits of twigs and leaves were clinging to her dark hair. She was wearing a loosely fitting shirtwaist and a man's—probably cast off by her father or a brother—faded duck pants upon which were bloodstains. Her calf-high black button shoes did not show much wear.

"Who are you? What's your name?" Bart asked gently, hearing Crockett come up and take a position behind him.

The girl frowned, and a bit of the fear faded from her eyes. "Meg . . . Meg," she murmured.

"Sure is kind of a pretty little thing," Reno said. "Was a man to wash off that dirt and dress her up in some female duds, why she'd be right easy to look at."

Foraker, aware then of his position on top of the girl as he sought to prevent her from escaping, rolled to one side and got to his feet.

"She's just a kid," he said, and reaching down, caught the girl by a hand and drew her upright. Smiling at her, he jerked a thumb at the outlaw.

"This is my pardner, Reno Crockett," he said, "and I'm called Bart Foraker."

Meg gave no sign that she understood, but continued to stare dully at the ground.

"Where were you—the wagon train—your folks headed?"

The girl shook her head, began to cry softly. She was still in shock, that was evident, but talking was probably the best remedy at the moment and Foraker pressed the point.

"The wagon train—where was it going?"

"Colorado—my uncle," Meg replied haltingly, and brushed at a wisp of her mahogany-colored hair that had strayed across a cheek.

As Reno had said, she actually was a right pretty girl despite her unkempt appearance, and the rough clothing she was wearing failed to conceal her well-developed figure. But she was young—probably no more than fifteen, Bart reckoned—and while girls along the frontier graduated into womanhood at an early age, thanks to circumstance and environment, Meg was still just a child as far as he was concerned.

"Where in Colorado?" he asked.

"San Luis—my uncle. We—we were moving there. To live with him—his family—a farm."

"Where are you from?" Foraker pressed, hopeful of keeping her talking.

"North Carolina—the hill country—"

Bart smiled, nodded. "Figured from your accent you came from somewhere in the South."

"North Carolina—the hill country," Meg repeated woodenly. "Going to Colorado—my—"

"Well, you sure ain't going there now," Crockett cut in, and glanced over his shoulder. "Come on, let's get the hell out of here."

The outlaw's harsh words seemed to release the strain, and pent-up emotions banked within the girl. Her face crumpled, a cry escaped her throat, and throwing herself onto Foraker, she wrapped her arms about his neck in a tight circle.

Crockett swore, grinned. "You got yourself another pardner," he said with a sly wink.

Foraker ignored the man. Having grown up with five sisters as well as three brothers in his Tennessee home, he recognized immediately the girl's need for comfort and reassurance.

Freeing one hand, he began to pat her gently on the shoulder all the while murmuring comforting words, but a question was rising in his mind—and in Reno Crockett's, too, he felt certain. In that next moment the outlaw voiced it.

"What're we going to do with the gal?"

"One thing for damn sure," Bart replied, faintly irritated by Reno's tone, "we can't ride off and leave her here!"

"Then what? If you're thinking to take her back up to Colorado you can flat out kiss Mexico good-bye because we'll be heading ourselves straight into that posse—or maybe a bunch of them Indians!"

At the mention of the braves Meg released her arms and drew away from Foraker. Fear again filled her eyes and her features became strained.

"Don't worry," he said, "they're gone."

"It was awful," the girl said, glancing around as if wishing to verify Bart's words. "The yelling, and shooting, and—and killing."

"Never mind that now. We can talk about it later if you want," Foraker said, quieting her.

He was puzzled as to how Meg had escaped the fate that overtook other members of the wagon train. Had she been off alone when the renegades struck? That didn't seem likely, for the pilgrims appeared not to be camped, but making their way across the arroyo at the time.

"We're plain damn fools to keep stalling around here," Crockett declared impatiently. "If you're figuring to keep the lady and take her along, then let's get started. If you ain't decided yet, let's move anyway—do our palavering somewhere else where them redskins ain't liable to find us."

"The lady, as you call her," Foraker said stiffly, "ain't but fourteen or maybe fifteen years old. Telling you now to watch what you say, and how you say it."

It occurred to Bart Foraker in that next moment that

32

the protective air he had assumed where the girl was concerned was a bit fatherly, and perhaps uncalled for. But it had surfaced naturally, without conscious thought, and he could see the situation in no other way.

Reno, however, was right; they should move on, not only to avoid encountering the Apaches, should they return, but to maintain a respectable distance between Sheriff Burke's posse and themselves. Bart had no illusions as to what would happen should the lawman and his deputies catch him again; this time he would find himself being hanged from the nearest tree. A similar fate would probably be accorded Crockett.

"We'll head south," Bart said. "There's some old Indian ruins on ten, maybe fifteen miles from here. Can camp there for the night while we figure what to do."

He glanced then to the west. The sun still hung above the range of towering mountains, and he reckoned they could reach the ruins well before dark. Taking the girl by the arm, he started to retrace his earlier steps through the brush. Meg hung back, fear and distrust again bright in her eyes.

"You best come with us," Foraker said gently.

"Hell, leave her stay if that's what she's wanting," Reno said. "We ain't got the time to fool with her."

"We'll take time," Bart snapped, and put his attention on Meg again. "You'll be all right—we'll look out for you."

The girl hesitated briefly, and then allowed Foraker to take her hand and lead her toward the horses. When they reached the open ground and she again saw the smoking remains of the wagons and their contents, the recollection of what had taken place once more set her to trembling.

"Ma—pa," she cried as tears began to stream down her face. "Where are—"

"They're dead," Foraker said as gently as he could. "They're all right now. We buried them, and the others."

Meg continued to weep quietly for several more moments, and then as if understanding and accepting, she went willingly with the two men to where the horses were tethered, and without protest took her place behind Foraker on his bay.

They moved off at once, following the faint dual tracks of a seldom-used road that cut its course across the empty flats in a southwesterly direction. They saw no one during the first miles, were alone except for an occasional prairie-dog village and a distant herd of antelope that raced along parallel to them like graceful, golden creatures out of some ancient legend.

"This here place where we're going—can we get water there? Ain't but a drop or two left in the canteens."

At Crockett's words Foraker said, "Hoping so. There's a spring that's usually running this time of year, but there's a chance it'll be dry."

"A chance, eh? Maybe we'll get water! Hell, we ought've headed for some other place where for sure there'd be water. Thought you said you knew this country."

"I know it's mostly dry. The last for-sure water was the Pecos River back up a ways—"

"I don't recollect crossing no rivers!" Reno cut in.

"We didn't. Was when we were sticking close to the brushy hills, dodging that posse," Foraker said, and as if the mention of Burke's party jogged his mind, he turned and cast a glance to the north.

Riders . . . they were well in the distance—too far, in fact, to count—but they were there. Whether it was the lawman and his posse or a band of Indians—or even a group of cowhands riding to some town, there was no way of knowing for certain. But it was best to assume the worst.

"Let's get these horses to moving," he said, making no mention of what he had seen. "I want to reach that spring and get settled before dark."

★ 6 ★

They reached the spring not long before dark and immediately set up camp. Meg, occasionally breaking into tears during the journey when she had thoughts of her parents and friends, went first to the water, knelt, and after satisfying her thirst, bathed her face, arms, and hands and did what she could to repair the damage to her clothing, all but torn from her body during the attack of the renegades.

She returned then to where Foraker had arranged stones for a cooking fire and was digging into the grub sack for items with which to prepare the evening meal.

"I—I can do that if you want me to," she said, dropping to her knees beside him. "You make the fire—and bring water for the coffee."

Foraker nodded, pleased that Meg had apparently shaken the stunned lethargy into which the Apache attack had plunged her. Permitting her to take over familiar duties would go far in restoring her self-assurance.

Turning away, Bart sought out a supply of dry wood and built a fire in the pit enclosed by the circle of rocks. Then, taking the coffeepot, he filled it from the spring, low but with an ample amount of water, and placed it over the flames. Meanwhile, Meg had filled the spider with strips of meat raggedly sliced with the bit of broken knife Foraker had salvaged at the scene of the Indian attack in the arroyo, and was adding other available foods to make a rich, tasty stew.

Crockett, having watered the horses and loosened their gear, had picketed them on a patch of grass just beyond the spring, and he was now settled on a rock at the edge of the camp, his attention on Meg as she went efficiently about her chore.

"That little gal would sure come in handy in more ways than one, going to Mexico," he said as Foraker, having removed the blanket roll from the back of his saddle, began to spread it out near the fire for Meg's later use.

"Too young. Said that before," Bart replied bluntly.

Reno laughed. "For a jasper what got throwed in the calaboose for just plain taking a woman you're mighty particular all of a sudden! Didn't figure your kind ever come across one too young—or too old, either."

Bart straightened with anger, and he had an urge to cross the camp swiftly and ram the words spoken by the outlaw back down the man's throat. Meg, too, had heard; she had paused in what she was doing and was staring thoughtfully into the fire.

"No call for you to say that, Reno," Foraker replied in a tight, barely controlled voice. "I had nothing to do with that told you before."

"Oh, sure," Crockett said easily. "Seems I do recollect you claiming you was innocent—that all them lawmen had made a big mistake."

"They did—and I'm aiming to prove it—someday."

"Good luck," Crockett said dryly. "But way it usually works out, a man never gets the chance to prove the law's wrong—which they ain't most of the time. . . . Now, what're we going to do about that girl? Smartest thing'll be for us to take her with us to Mexico—be right good company and a lot of help—but you ain't for that, I can see."

"No—"

"Then what?"

Meg, continuing to put together a stew from the meager stock of provisions she found in the grub sack—a chore she had performed, or helped perform, daily for months, it seemed to her—listened to the conversation between the two men. They argued continuously, she had noticed, with things usually going Bart Foraker's way.

Meg was glad of that. She didn't like Reno Crockett much, had turned instinctively to Foraker for comfort and protection.

The horror of the Apache attack still filled her mind, but as women of great strength will do, she had pushed it off into one corner where—never to be forgotten—it would not cloud the necessity for meeting the present with everyday practicality.

"The dead's dead, and the living's got to go on living," she'd heard her pa say more than once, and it occurred to her now just how much truth there was in the old axiom. No matter what, she must go on—just how and where apparently was up to the two strangers who had entered her life.

But no matter what they decided, it would be better than what she had been faced with when the Indians attacked the wagon train. A shudder passed through her as the horrifying, frightful moments filled her thoughts again.

They had gotten an early start that morning, which pleased her pa; one of the other families, the Gilchrists, had become a bit slothful of late, probably because they were tired, and there had been numerous delays on their account.

But this day looked to be one in which they would cover considerable ground. She, with her parents, had taken the lead position in their wagon, and were being followed by the Gilchrist's, after whom came the Webbs, with Damian, their son, who'd just had his twenty-first birthday, doing the driving.

It was around midmorning when they were crossing a wide, dry wash that the Indians came yelling and screeching out of the brush that lined one side of it. The men hardly had time to grab their weapons before the braves were upon them—some using rifles, others bows and arrows, spears, and stone hatchets.

Her father was one of the first to die, her mother only moments later. And the next thing after that, Meg found herself being yanked off the seat and thrown to the ground. She remembered an Indian standing over her, dark body glistening with sweat, eyes filled with a wildness, hideous painted face turned down to her. He raised his hatchet—or tomahawk, as she'd heard it called—for a blow that would have split her head, but he paused.

Extending an arm, he grasped the front of her shirtwaist and ripped it open. A grin parted his thick lips, exposed broad, yellowed teeth, and turning, he yelled something to the other savages, who were by then ransacking the trunks and bags removed from the wagons, which had been overturned and were burning. The horses, still in their harness, were being led off into the brush.

The brave towering over her thrust his hatchet into a braided leather belt he was wearing over a breechcloth, and bending over he caught her by the arms, hung her over a shoulder, and moved off after the horses. Frantic, frightened beyond belief, she had screamed and fought to free herself from the Apache, but her efforts had gone for nothing. A powerful, muscular man, he handled her as easily as if she were a small child.

Meg, with the chilling yells of the Indians as they

made sport of their easy victory echoing in her ears, had a glimpse of her parents sprawled on the sandy ground not far from their burning wagon. On beyond them were the Gilchrists, lying side by side. She didn't see the older Webbs, but Damian, who'd asked her to marry him after they reached Colorado and she became seventeen, was huddled against the end of the family vehicle. Blood was bubbling from a gaping wound in his chest, and he seemed unaware of the flames that were enveloping the wagon and creeping toward him. His gun, a long-barreled squirrel rifle, lay across his knees.

"Damian!" she had screamed in desperation as the brave carried her toward the brush.

He had raised his head at her cry, and then a moment or so later, her captor had stumbled and gone down, and she realized that Damian, probably with his last breath and ounce of strength, had gotten off a shot. The ball had struck the Indian in the leg, Meg supposed—she was too frightened to take note, knew only that the Apache was hit and, in an attempt to save himself from falling, had loosened his grip on her.

She had thrown herself from the man instantly and, spurred by overwhelming fear and the angry shouts of the brave, had raced blindly off into the brush. Minutes later, breathless, she had found a place among the rocks and dense growth used evidently as a lair by some wild animal, and crawling into it, she had covered herself with leaves and dead branches.

A time later two braves had passed close by, no doubt in search of her. Neither was the one who had carried her from the wagon, and she guessed he had been so badly wounded by Damian Webb's bullet that he was unable to take part in the hunt. The Apaches apparently didn't feel she was worth spending too much time on, since she would not belong to them if found; and also perhaps fearing the arrival of more immigrants, they soon gave up and returned to the others. Not long after they had disappeared, the entire party, leading the wagon horses, passed by no more than a dozen strides from where she lay hidden.

Meg couldn't recall much of what she had done after that. When the Indians had gone, a sort of stunned lassitude overtook her, and she simply remained where she was in the evil-smelling lair unable to think or do anything other than to continue hiding.

And then a time later she heard voices—men's voices speaking her language. At first the sound came from where the wagons had been attacked, then from somewhere close as if the men—two of them, she thought—were making certain there were no more Indians around.

When they had returned to the big wash and she realized from what they said that they were burying the dead, she crept out of her concealment and, as if prompted by some inner compulsion, made her way to where she could watch. It was all hazy, like a terrifying bad dream, and she'd had difficulty fully understanding what had taken place and what was now happening.

Shortly she'd found herself again prone on the ground, being held there by one of the two men. She hadn't remembered running from him or being caught, but undoubtedly it was so.

Meg, stirring the thick stew that now filled the night air with its savory odor, was glad she had not escaped from the two men; otherwise, she would still be back there in the thick brush with little hope of surviving and most likely ending up in the hands of the Apaches again.

Portioning out the stew into the two tin plates she had found, intending to eat her own share from the frying pan itself, she called to the men—apparently still discussing her fate—and advised them that the meal was ready.

What they had decided she could only guess, but Meg hoped she would end up with the younger of the pair—Bart Foraker. The other one, Crockett, chilled her blood every time he looked at her. There were two kinds of men in this world, her mother had said: the ones who respect a woman, and the kind who only want to use them. Reno Crockett, it was easy to see, belonged in the latter group.

★ 7 ★

"That sure does smell good, little lady," Reno said, smacking his lips loudly as he took up his plate, grinning appreciatively at Meg. Helping himself to a chunk of bread, he nodded at Foraker.

"Telling you again she'd be mighty handy to have along with us."

Foraker only shrugged and, with his plate filled with stew and a cup of coffee in hand, dropped to his heels upwind of the fire and began to eat. Meg, making use of the frying pan for a plate, moved in beside him, and with a sharpened stick for a fork quietly began to enjoy her meal.

"We ain't asked her what she'd like to do," Reno continued between mouthfuls of bread sopped into the thick mixture. "Why don't we let her tell us her choosings?"

Bart glanced at the girl. "You feel like talking?"

Her shoulders stirred slightly. "I guess so—"

Foraker said, "Good. Expect that means you're feeling better. . . . You told us part of your name—Meg. What's the rest of it?"

"Swope. My pa was Lewis Swope. We were all moving to Colorado—San Luis. Pa's brother has a farm there. He aimed to get some land and start farming too."

"Ask her about going along with us," Reno prompted. "Can forget all this beating around the bush."

43

"Who were the other folks with you?" Foraker asked, coolly ignoring the outlaw.

"The Gilchrists and the Webbs. They planned to get farms around San Luis, too. I was probably going to marry Damian Webb when I got to be seventeen."

"How old are you now?"

"Almost fifteen . . . Damian saved me. He shot the Indian who was carrying me off," Meg said, and went into a brief narration of the morning's events.

She told it calmly, breaking down only once, when she related the deaths of her parents. The speed with which it had all happened had served as a sort of anesthetic cloaking the grisly details and undoubtedly impressing them to a lesser extent on her mind.

"You want to go with us to Mexico?" Crockett asked bluntly when she had finished.

Meg was staring into the fire, now slowly dwindling. Overhead the sky was masking itself with dark, scudding clouds, and the smell of rain was in the cool air.

"I'd like to go to my uncle's," she replied hesitantly.

Reno swore. "Hell, sister, we can't do that! We can't go backtracking in that direction—just wouldn't be healthy for us!"

Meg resumed her eating, soft features expressionless.

Bart reached out, touched her on the shoulder. "Don't worry—we'll get you to San Luis—"

"Maybe you will!" Crockett exploded. "But don't go ringing me in on it! I ain't no damn fool!"

"Suit yourself," Bart murmured, taking a swallow of his coffee.

The outlaw moved up to the fire, refilled his cup from the pot. "Why the hell don't we just keep going on south and drop her off at the first town we come to?"

"Las Vegas is behind us," Foraker said. "If we double back that far we might as well go all the way to San Luis. And El Paso is a far piece on ahead."

44

"Ain't there no towns between here and there?"

"Not on the trail we're following—we're dodging towns, in case you've forgot. Besides, if there was, do you think it would be right to just turn Meg here loose in a strange place—a young, pretty girl with nobody to look out for her?"

"We could hand her over to a sheriff or a town marshal, and let him—" Crockett began, and then broke off, realizing what he had said: for either of them to seek out a lawman would be inviting arrest, for by that time word of their escape undoubtedly had been received by every law officer in the area.

"Maybe we could find us a preacher and turn her over to him—that's sort of their job, you know, looking after widows and orphans and such," Reno continued. "You know damn well, was we to head back north with her, our goose'll be cooked because that damned posse will nail us sure."

"Posse?" Meg repeated. "Is there someone after you?"

"A big one—a sheriff and about a dozen deputies—and maybe a U.S. marshal. We busted out of a jail and are trying our damnedest to get to Mexico before they nab us. That's why we're in such a powerful hurry."

Meg set down the pan she was holding, a deep frown pulling at her features. "I heard you talking about not wanting to turn back, but I didn't know the reason," she said. "I—I don't want to cause you any trouble. If you'll just take me to the nearest town, leave me, I'll find a way to get to my uncle's place."

"Now, that's what I'm wanting to hear," Crockett exclaimed. "You're plenty smart, little lady. You just trail along with us till we come to some town, and then—"

"Forget it, Reno," Foraker cut in sharply. "We're taking her to San Luis—leastwise, I am. You can come along or you can keep on going south—I aim to see this

45

girl gets to where she wants to go without anything more happening to her."

Reno Crockett threw his cup to the ground angrily. "The hell you say! All right, you just go right ahead, put a rope around your neck—I'm going on to Mexico."

Foraker rose and, making no reply, began to collect the pans and dishes for washing in the spring. Meg Swope immediately joined him, and together they crossed to the pool of water and there, with the aid of the sand along the edge of the pond, cleaned the utensils. When they were finished and ready to return to the camp, the girl laid a hand on Bart's arm.

"I don't want to cause trouble between you and your friend," she said hesitantly.

Foraker shrugged. "I'd hardly call him a friend. Just happened we got thrown together and are heading—or were—for the same place."

"Will it be risky for you to take me to Colorado—like he says?"

Again Foraker's shoulders stirred. " 'Long as I keep my eyes peeled it'll be all right."

"If there's a chance that you could get caught by that sheriff, I won't let you do it—you can just leave me at the next town."

"Can forget that. I'll see that you get to your uncle's place—and don't spend time worrying over me; I've been looking out for myself for a lot of years."

Meg smiled, and even in the poor light Bart could see how it lit up her features and brought out her beauty.

"A lot of years," she repeated softly. "You can't be all that old! Why I'll bet you're not much older than I am!"

"I reckon I've got a few years on you," Foraker said, glancing up at the sky now closing in as the meshing clouds continued to unite and form a thick overcast. He

46

actually wasn't much older than Meg, he supposed—five or six years—but that could mean much.

Over toward Pendernal Mountain a wolf howled forlornly and was answered almost immediately by one of his kind somewhere nearby.

"Best you get some rest," Foraker said, starting back to the camp. "Be a hard day tomorrow . . . I fixed a blanket for you."

"That's your bed," Meg said at once, protesting. "I don't mind sitting by the fire."

"Won't be any fire—Indians might spot it, or maybe somebody else. And don't fret none about me. I've spent many a night with only my brush jacket for a cover."

"By hell, it's about time," Crockett greeted them as they came into the small circle of light being cast by the dying fire. "Figured maybe you two was just going to spend the night down there in the bushes. I'm betting she was real good, being young and—"

Reno never finished what he intended to say. Bart Foraker dropped the pans he was carrying and, lunging forward, drove a fist into the outlaw's jaw.

Crockett cursed, staggered back, and sat down hard. Foraker was on him instantly. Seizing the man by the shirt front, he cocked his arm for a second punishing blow. Reno threw up both hands, palms forward.

"Back off! Back off!" he shouted, blood seeping from a corner of his mouth. "I didn't mean nothing."

"The hell you didn't," Foraker snarled, relaxing slightly as he released his grip on the outlaw. "I know exactly what you meant—and so do you."

"Well, was only that you was gone so long with her out there in the dark—and knowing how you are with women, I—"

Again Foraker's arm came back. His fist once more became a rock-hard knot. "You know better than that, Crockett!"

47

The outlaws hands were a protective shield before his face for a second time. "All right, all right! I know better, but it sure was looking like you and her—"

"I don't give a damn what you think it looked like," Foraker raged. "And I won't have you shooting off your mouth about it again—hear?"

Crockett nodded. "Sure, I hear," he said, smirking. "I'm smart enough not to go horning in on another man's private property."

Anger again heightened in Bart Foraker, and once more he made a move to smash his fist into the outlaw's face, but he paused. What was the point? With the kind of mind Reno had, he'd never convince the man that his interest in Meg Swope lay purely in the nature of help for the girl. Anyway, Crockett would head out on his own in the morning, and chances were they'd never meet again.

"Come daylight, we'll split the grub, and you can keep going for Mexico," Foraker said coldly. "Meg and I'll be turning north to Colorado."

★ 8 ★

With the morning's sunrise came the first splatter of rain—small, hard drops that spurted dust as they fiercely hammered the dry, thirsty land and danced merrily when they struck the placid surface of the spring.

But it was only a brief shower, failing even to slow the process of breakfast, prepared by Meg and eaten in silence by all. Only when they had finished was there any conversation.

"Want you to take what grub you figure you'll need," Foraker said, gesturing at Crockett, "and move on. Happens we're only a couple of days or so from Las Vegas. We'll stock up when we get there."

Reno wagged his head skeptically. "You're forgetting you ain't got no cash, or no guts for busting into some store, either. Anyway, you'll be a damn fool to show your face in a town big as Vegas. Somebody'll spot you sure."

"I'll manage," Foraker replied quietly. "Get your share—I want to head out soon as I can."

Crockett hunched over the grub sack, dug around a bit, and selected a portion of the stock it contained, all of which he stuffed into his saddlebags. That done, he swung up onto his horse.

"So long, pardner. I figure you're making a hell of a mistake, but you ain't one a man can get anywhere ar-

49

guing with. If you get out of this with a whole hide, look me up in Mexico."

"Big country," Foraker said indifferently, and picking up the grub sack and taking a hitch in its neck, hung it on his saddle.

"Yeh, expect it is—and I ain't even sure how to get there."

"Just keep riding south, and you'll come to it," Bart said, and nodded to Meg. "We're ready to go."

The girl stepped quickly up to the waiting bay and, with Foraker assisting, settled in behind the cantle of the hull. As Bart mounted, Crockett spoke.

"Good luck—"

"Same to you," Foraker responded without feeling, watching the outlaw cut his black about and ride off at a leisurely trot.

Bart sat motionless for several moments, glance on the outlaw, and then with Meg pressing against him, arms partly encircling his waist as she sought to steady herself, he put the bay into an easy lope.

The big horse had enjoyed the night's rest as well as satisfying himself on the good grass and fresh water, and was in fine fettle and anxious to run. But Foraker held him back; the bay was carrying double, and while the extra load was not noticeable to him then, it would become so as the day wore on. Bart was hopeful of covering considerable ground before sunset, so he didn't want the gelding to tire himself out too soon.

They rode on through the cool, early hours. The rain came again, showering from the overcast but for only a few minutes. It made for a pleasant passage across the rolling flats and slopes vivid with acre upon acre of purple asters, the varying yellows of pingwing, snakeweed, and prickly poppy, the lush green of freshly washed grass, which contrasted agreeably with the darker shades of the sturdy piñon and juniper trees.

"This land is so pretty—so beautiful," Meg murmured. "You'd never think something—something like what happened to my folks would be possible."

"Pretty all right," Foraker admitted, "but dangerous, too. Never pays to let down your guard—not for a minute. If the country itself doesn't turn on you—a big sandstorm in the summer or a killing blizzard in the winter—the Indians will."

Bart paused to look back over the course they had taken. He was following no set trail, but was choosing a route that kept them close to the hills where brush was plentiful and offered concealment if necessary.

"Those mountains over to the west—to the left— they're the Manzanos. Look fine now but the snow gets plenty deep in the winter. Been more than one man caught there in a sudden storm who didn't make it out. Same goes for the higher mountains you see on ahead— the Sandias they're called. And the Sangre de Cristos. We'll be seeing them when we get close to Las Vegas."

Again Bart Foraker threw a glance over a shoulder. He had an uncomfortable feeling that they were being followed, although twice now he had looked back and seen no one.

"My uncle said it would be cold in Colorado—"

"He's plenty right. Ain't much level ground up there. Most all high mountain country."

"It's gets cold in North Carolina, too— What's the matter? Is there something wrong?"

Foraker had veered abruptly from course in behind a thick clump of brush and halted. Dismounting, he drew his pistol.

"Something just keeps telling me we've got somebody trailing us."

At once Meg slid from the back of the bay. Fear heightened her color and widened her eyes. "Indians— do you think it's Indians?"

51

"Can't be sure. We'll stay put right here till we know for certain. Could be only—"

Foraker's voice broke off suddenly as the steady thud of an oncoming horse reached him. Pushing Meg farther back into the shadows, gun ready, he crouched lower. Abruptly he drew himself upright and slid his weapon back into its holster.

"Crockett," he said in a voice filled with irritation, and stepped out to meet the outlaw.

"Changed my thinking," Reno said cheerfully as he came to a halt. "Come to me that you oughtn't to be making it up through here alone, just blundering along blind like. Two guns are a lot better'n one, so—"

"Expect what you ought to be saying is that you got cold feet about going to Mexico, was afraid you'd get yourself lost, or maybe caught by some lawman."

Reno pulled off his hat, grinned broadly. "Well, now, you just could be right. Where's the little gal?"

Meg stepped out into the open. The outlaw nodded and said, "Howdy, little lady. You're looking peart. Was it you that seen me a-coming?"

The girl shook her head.

Foraker said, "Got the feeling we were being trailed. Ducked in here to wait and see who it was. This saying you changed your mind—that mean you're wanting to throw in with us again?"

"Yep, sure does. I reckon you're still heading for Colorado—or are you going to Las Vegas and turning her over to somebody there to—"

"Not going to Las Vegas unless I have to. Figure to head straight for Colorado, and San Luis."

Crockett sighed heavily. "Hell, was hoping you'd hashed this over and was going to do what I said, but can see you ain't. You're as hardheaded as any mule I ever come across—meaning no offense! It all right if I join up with you?"

"Your choice, only if you do, it's on my terms—"

"Meaning what by that?"

"We'll do it my way, and you'll watch your mouth."

"Sure, sure," Crockett said, and cast a glance at the threatening sky. "You reckon the rain's over? If it keeps coming and going, I'll be plenty wet before dark."

Foraker said nothing, but helped Meg back onto the bay—this time putting her in the saddle while he swung up behind. She looked at him, puzzled by the change.

"Figured you'd be tired of straddling those saddlebags, and I'd best spell you off."

Meg smiled and shook her head. "No, was doing fine. And you ought to be up here where you can see better."

"He can see what he wants," Crockett stated with a broad grin. "Don't worry none about him; he's right where—"

The outlaw broke off as Foraker, urging the bay forward, chilled him with an angry look.

"Was only meaning—"

"I don't give a hoot what you meant—just keep your lip buttoned and maybe we'll get along," Bart snapped as they resumed a northward course along the brushy fringe of the hills.

He was sorry Reno Crockett had changed his mind and rejoined Meg and him. Not only did the outlaw continually rankle him with his sly insinuations, but it would have been much easier to make their way across the land without him. A solitary horse—even one with two riders—was less noticeable. He could tell Reno to turn around, strike off on his own, and leave Meg and him alone, he supposed; but, as Crockett had pointed out, two guns were better than one if . . .

"You looking off toward them trees to the right?" Reno called from his position a stride or so to the rear. "If you ain't, you sure better."

Bart shifted his attention to the point the outlaw had

indicated. He swore softly under his breath. A dozen riders—coming almost directly for them.

"Indians," he said, and turned to look ahead where a deep, brush-filled arroyo sliced the land before them.

"Don't think they've seen us yet. Let's get down in that wash—fast!"

★ 9 ★

Spurring the bay, Foraker cut deeper into the brush along which they were passing, and hurriedly guided the big horse down into the welter of thick growth in the arroyo a dozen yards away. Mumbling curses and reminders to Bart that such was just what he'd predicted should they be foolish enough to turn back, Reno Crockett followed.

Reaching the depths of the cut, Foraker, not bothering to swing his leg over in the customary dismount, pushed himself off the back of the bay's rump and ran quickly to where he could see the party of oncoming braves.

"Still heading straight for us," he said aloud, and swore quietly. He at first had thought the Indians would likely keep to the trail they were apparently following—one that would take them away from the arroyo; it now looked as if they planned to use the arroyo itself as a path.

Returning to where Meg, now out of the saddle, and Crockett, also off his horse, were waiting, he hurriedly outlined their situation. The outlaw's reaction was what Bart expected.

"Hell—we should've stayed up there on the flat! Could've maybe cut back, hid out somewheres. Down here we're trapped good!"

55

"Up on the flat, no matter which way we'd gone, they would've spotted us," Foraker said.

Meg, face drawn, hands clenched so tightly at her sides that the knuckles were white, said nothing, but Bart knew that fear was racing through her as she recalled again the incident back in another arroyo where she had lost her parents and friends at the hands of Indians.

"Let's get ready for them," Foraker said, laying a reassuring hand on the girl's shoulder. "Looks like a-plenty of rocks and brush on down a ways. We'll move, make a stand there."

Without waiting for agreement or objection from Reno, Bart took up the reins of his horse, and with Meg Swope at his side, hastily changed positions to where a finger of dense growth and jumbled rocks extended out into the wash.

Working well into the center of the ragged formation, Foraker immediately secured his horse to a stout clump of rabbit brush.

"Be a good place there to fort up," he said, pointing to a small clearing in the center of the area as Crockett tethered his black alongside the bay. "But we'd better lay more brush across the front—screen it a bit heavier."

Wheeling, he trotted a short distance down the arroyo and halted near where several dry bushes, dead for some cause, offered a source.

Ripping out a half a dozen or more of the clumps, he came about, found both Meg and Reno waiting to help. Motioning for them to gather up what they could, all doubled back to the clearing. Carefully, taking pains to show no unusual break in the natural growth, they inserted the bushes along the north side of the clearing, thus further screening their hiding place from the Indians who would be passing by only a few yards away.

That done, Foraker glanced about and nodded. "Not

much more we can do," he said, and crossed to a small rise where he could have a view of the country to the east. The braves, much nearer, were still bearing directly toward them.

"Time we got set," he said, rejoining the others. "Best thing—"

"They getting close?" Crockett asked.

Bart said, "Yes," and then continued, "Started to say we've got to get down low—flat on the ground. If luck's with us, they'll ride on by without ever knowing we're here."

"What about them horses?" Reno wondered. "Standing up like they are, ain't them redskins going to spot them?"

"We'll have to throw them down and hold their heads. Bay of mine's had it done to him before so I don't think he'll give us a problem. Don't know about the horse you're riding."

"I'll put him down—and keep him quiet," Crockett declared. Then, in an angry voice, added, "Damn it all to hell, how do I always wind up in some kind of a lousy picklement? I'm wishing now I'd kept going for Mexico."

Foraker grinned at the outlaw's frustration. "Maybe you just wanted to be with friends," he drawled, and ignoring Crockett's quick retort, turned his attention to the flats in the east and listened intently.

"Not far," he said, settling back. "Can hear them talking. Best we throw the horses and get them quieted."

Stepping to where the two animals were tied, Bart freed the bay's lines, led him into the clearing, and by drawing the animal's neck sharply to one side, caused him to fall. With the bay prone, he at once moved to where he could keep the horse's head down by pressing it firmly to the ground. Close by, Reno Crockett was go-

57

ing through an identical maneuver with the black he was riding.

"I reckon he's going to behave," the outlaw said, breathing a bit hard from his efforts. "Just hope he won't get nervous and try to get up."

"Not likely if you keep his head pinned down and sort of pet him—rub him along the neck."

"We could be doing all this damn work for nothing," Crockett declared impatiently. "Hell, we've got two guns—why don't we just open up on them gut-eaters, blow their damned heads off?"

"Thought of that—too many of them," Foraker replied. "There's a dozen, maybe fifteen braves in the party. We'd get a few of them, but not all. They'd scatter, circle, and come in on us from all sides. We'd not have a chance."

Crockett's horse began to struggle—kicking its legs and thrashing wildly about. The outlaw cursed, pressed more firmly on the animal's head, and then, taking Foraker's suggestion, began to stroke the black's neck while speaking to him in a low voice.

A high, shrill yell broke the hush. Laughter and shouting followed. Foraker drew his pistol and crouched lower.

"Stay down," he whispered, "and pray that horse doesn't start cutting up again."

Crockett had also pulled his weapon from its holster, now had it lying on the ground nearby. More yells split the quiet, and once there was a sudden, quick pound of hooves as one of the braves made a rush at something.

"There they are," Foraker warned softly.

The Indians became visible through the curtain of brush. Fifteen by count, they were leading three horses, no doubt stolen from some rancher or homesteader or taken in a raid. The thinly shrouded sun glistened dully off the braves' curved, slack bodies, paint streaked their faces, and their jet-black hair was held in place with a band of cloth that circled their heads.

"Careful," Foraker cautioned.

The party was now directly opposite the clearing, riding slowly. Some of the Apaches were hunched low over their plodding horses, apparently dozing. Others were laughing, gesturing, and talking back and forth, making much of something that had occurred. Abruptly one of the younger braves threw back his head and filled the air with a nerve-shattering yell.

The tension was too much for Meg Swope. Crouched beside Foraker, she suddenly broke into quiet sobbing and crowded closer to him. Laying aside the pistol he was holding, Bart put his arm about the girl and comforted her as best he could. Had his other arm been free and not engaged in holding down the bay, he would have embraced Meg completely.

Several of the sleeping Indians, jarred to wakefulness by the exultant brave, shouted angrily at him. He responded with another yell that echoed along the arroyo, and then began to laugh. At that moment Crockett's horse once again started to struggle. Foraker released the girl and took up his pistol as tension rose within him.

One of the Apaches, apparently having heard the noise set up by the horse, quickly quieted by Reno, turned his head and stared at the wall of brush. Bart felt Meg stiffen. He glanced down at her, forced a reassuring smile to his lips. She seemed to take courage from that and, pressing closer to him, put a hand to her mouth as if to stifle any sound that might unwillingly escape her throat.

The brave settled back, evidently not too interested in whatever it had been that had drawn his attention. The band had been on a raid that night before, Foraker guessed, and gone without sleep, and most all were tired.

"They're going on by," Crockett said, a thread of relief in his voice.

"We were lucky," Bart added, feeling the tension slowly drain from his body. "Glad you saw them in time for us to get set. . . . Better hold off moving until they're a mile or so away."

"Just hope I can," the outlaw replied. "This nag's getting mighty spooky."

The black proved to be of no trouble, and after the Apaches were a safe distance away, Foraker and Crockett got to their feet, brought the horses upright, and prepared to move on. Meg, shaken by the taut experience, silently took her place behind the cantle of Foraker's saddle, waited until he had mounted, and then, as they started forward, put her arms about his waist and hugged him tightly to show her relief and express her thanks.

"I was so scared," she murmured.

"Reckon we all were," Bart said. "Was a close one—too close, if you ask me."

"I—I don't know what I would have done if I'd been by myself and they'd come along—"

"You would have managed just like you did before—stayed hidden until they were gone," Foraker said. "But don't go stewing about what might have been. Never does a body any good."

Meg was silent for several moments. Then, "Do you think we'll run into more of them—the Indians?"

"Hard to say. All we can do is keep a sharp watch and quick get out of sight if we do."

"Goes for that posse, too," Crockett reminded. "Like as not they've got scouts scattered all over this part of the country looking for us."

"Can bet on it," Bart agreed as they pressed on

beneath the cloudy sky, following, as before, a course that kept them near the brush. "We spot even one rider anywhere, we best take cover."

But the day wore on without their steady progress being interrupted, and when darkness began to rise and shadows to form, Foraker turned toward a grove of cottonwoods a short distance to their right, where he figured there was the likelihood of a spring, for them to pitch night camp.

He guessed right. There was water—as there usually is where bright-leafed cottonwood trees grow strong and healthy—bubbling out of the reddish soil in the heart of the grove. They halted there and dismounted. As before, Crockett saw to the horses while Foraker, choosing a well-hidden spot for the small cook fire that would be necessary, searched about for smokeless dry wood; Meg, as before, assumed the cooking chores.

All were weary from the long day and from the tension brought about by the encounter with the Apache raiding party, and they were ready to turn in as soon as the meal was over.

Hunched near the low flames of the flickering fire, drinking a final cup of Meg's good coffee, Foraker watched the girl lay out her blanket near a heavily loaded gooseberry bush growing near the spring. The horses were picketed a short distance away, having watered, and now were grazing contentedly on the thick grass beneath the spreading trees.

"Ain't too far from Vegas," Crockett said. "You aim to stop there?"

Foraker took a swallow from his cup. "Too risky," he said with a shake of his head. "Can bet the law knows all about us and is on the watch."

"Just what I was thinking. But maybe we could—"

The outlaw's voice broke off as Foraker, constantly alert, raised a hand for silence. A sound in the brush nearby had caught his attention. Motioning a warning to Crockett, he set his cup on one of the rocks surrounding the fire pit and let his hand settle gently on the butt of the pistol at his hip. Reno, features indefinite in the weak light, also reached casually for his weapon. Instantly a voice challenged them from the depths of the surrounding brush.

"Hold it there, gents! We've got you covered. You make another move toward them irons you're wearing, and you're dead!"

Foraker's jaw tightened. Crockett swore deeply, remained motionless, while Meg, the blanket she intended to wrap about her still on the ground, did not stir.

Shortly a squat figure stepped out of the shadows. At about the same time a second and a third man appeared from nearby. All were hard-bitten, rough-looking riders with guns ready in their hands. Outlaws of the worst kind—there could be no doubt of it, Bart Foraker thought, casting a worried look at Meg.

★ 10 ★

"How about you two jaspers raising your hands while Hobie there dehorns you?" the man in the center ordered as he moved in closer. "John Willie, throw some wood on that fire so's we can see what we got."

John Willie, a young-looking man, tall, lean, with sun-darkened features, crossed quickly and, picking up a handful of dry branches, tossed them into the fire. As it sprang to life with a resulting flare of light, he saw the girl.

"Hey—lookee here!" he said in a voice that marked him as a Texan. "We done gone and caught us a little quail!"

The man called Hobie, at that moment reaching down to relieve Crockett of his pistol, paused and looked around. "Well, now, that sure is a comforting thought— say, what do you know, Ben—this here gent's an old pard of ours, Reno Crockett!"

Ben stepped in nearer, peered down at the outlaw. "Reno! That sure enough you?"

"Sure is," Crockett answered, and thrust out his hand. "I'm right pleased to see you again."

"Same here. Hell, I figured you'd been strung up years ago. . . . Can forget about taking his iron, Hobie, he's all right. Reckon that'll go for his pardner, too. . . . Who's the gal belong to, Reno, you?"

Foraker relaxed slightly, somewhat relieved that his

gun was not to be taken from him. Evidently the men knew Reno and were friends of his—or at least two of them were. The Texan had made no sign of recognition.

"Well, I reckon she don't belong to nobody, if you're meaning is she married, but my pard there, Bart Foraker, is sort of taking care of her."

"She ain't his woman?"

"Nope, could be I reckon, 'cepting he figures she's only a kid. . . . Want you to meet Bart."

"Sure thing," the one called Ben said, and moved to where Foraker sat. Extending his hand, he added, "Name's Ben Gilley. Other two boys're Hobie Green and John Willie Poe."

Foraker nodded coolly to the others. Gilley, a blond, pop-eyed, peeled-looking man, rubbed at his jaw. "You got your rope on that gal?"

"I'm looking after her, like Reno said, seeing to it that she gets where she wants to go."

"I see," Gilley said, and turned to Reno. "Don't suppose you got any drinking liquor?"

"Sure ain't," Crockett replied. "Where you headed?"

"No place special," Gilley said, and gestured at the Texan. "John Willie, you bring up the horses, tie them along with the others. . . . There any coffee left in that there pot? We done ate, but we didn't have nothing but water to drink."

"Meg'll make you some," Reno volunteered as the young Texan moved off into the woods for their mounts.

The girl glanced at Foraker. He nodded. He was not happy with the way things were shaping up, but it seemed best to go along with them for the time being.

Hobie Green, narrow-faced, with a hooknose, squatted beyond the fire, his eyes on Meg. "You on the run, Reno?" he asked, not shifting his attention.

64

"Yeh—both of us. Posse around here somewheres right now hunting us. We'd been pretty close to Mexico right now—that's where we was headed—when we come across the gal and had to turn around and head back. Redskins massacred her folks."

"What's the law after you for—a shooting?"

Reno nodded. "Yeh, put a slug in a jasper up Trinidad way. Foraker there was in for raping some rancher's wife, then choking her to death."

"That so?" Gilley said in a rising voice. "Guess I savvy now why he's so all-fired het up to keep that little gal for hisself."

"I had nothing to do with the murder of that woman," Bart said, coming to his feet. "Told you that before, Reno, telling you again—same as I did that sheriff."

Crockett laughed. It was apparent that he had switched allegiance, was throwing in with his old friends. "Yeh, every man I ever seen that was in jail claimed he was innocent. . . . What've you been doing, Ben? They had you locked up?"

Ben, squatting by the fire, eyes hungrily following Meg's every move, nodded. "Me and the boys just got let out. Put in three years for jumping a stagecoach and helping ourselves."

John Willie returned after bringing up their mounts and picketing them with the bay and Reno's black. He halted by the fire, joined in watching Meg as she went about preparing a fresh pot of coffee. When the girl leaned over to place the blackened container over the fire, he reached out and patted her on the buttocks. Meg jerked away and shrank close to Bart.

"Man, ain't she something!" John Willie marveled.

"Back off, mister," Foraker snapped, putting his arm protectively around the girl. "She's just a kid."

"Kid, hell!" Ben Gilley laughed. "Shaped up like she

65

is, I'm betting she's closer to eighteen—maybe even older!"

"You're wrong," Bart countered. "She's not even fifteen."

John Willie laughed. "Well, I always say if they're big enough, they're old enough," he drawled.

"Now, down where I come from," Hobie Green added, coming to his feet, "we stand them in a rain barrel. If they can see over the top they're big enough to bed."

"She's sure big enough for that," Ben Gilley observed, and stepping in closer to the girl, reached for the front of her shirtwaist. "You ain't never told us what to call you, girlie."

"Never mind," Foraker broke in roughly, pushing Ben's hand away. "I'm telling you again, leave her alone."

In the next moment Bart staggered back as Hobie Green, coming in from the side, shoved him away. "Best you just go see to the horses or something, mister, keep out from underfoot."

Foraker, grim set, caught his balance. Moving fast, he closed in on Green, now adding his efforts to those of Gilley in tearing off the girl's clothing. Bart's knotted fist struck the outlaw on the side of the head, sent him stumbling into Ben Gilley.

A yell went up as Hobie rocked to his left and went to his knees. Foraker, a combination of anger and fear for Meg's safety rushing through him, crowded in on the hooknosed outlaw. As Green came to his feet, he drove a second blow into the man, but Hobie had seen it coming and took it on the shoulder.

"Get him," Ben Gilley shouted. "Get the son of a bitch, Hobie!"

Green, head low, spun and charged. Foraker stepped quickly to his right and sent a sledgelike blow to the side

66

of the man's jaw. Hobie yelled in pain, but he did not go down, simply hung there, arms dangling, half-crouched. And then, a curse ripping from his mouth, he spun to meet Foraker.

Bart, waiting in the thin haze of dust that their scuffling boots had raised, straightened the outlaw with a hard uppercut and sent him reeling back. Blood was now trickling from the corners of his mouth, and he was sucking hard for wind.

"You're sure set on keeping that gal for yourself, ain't you, friend?"

It was Ben Gilley. Foraker half-turned, faced the outlaw.

"Well, best you get this in your head—this here time you're going to do some sharing—"

A shocking blow to the belly doubled Bart forward as Hobie took advantage of the distraction. He tried to pivot to get away from Green, now swarming all over him, and failed. Fists began to hammer at his head and face. A booted foot came from somewhere—Gilley's, he thought—smashed into his ribs, and sent a wave of pain shooting through him. A hard jolt to the jaw sent lights flashing in his head, and a moment later he realized he was down on hands and knees.

The rain of blows and periodic kicks ceased. He looked up. Everybody except Reno—and, of course, Meg—had taken a hand in the fight, it appeared.

Ben Gilley grinned down at him. "You ready to do some sharing, like I said?" he asked. "Or do you want me and the boys to do a little more convincing?"

Foraker lowered his head, stared at the ground. He for damn sure couldn't fight all three of the outlaws, that was certain—just as it was equally clear he'd get no help from Reno Crockett. And beaten to a pulp or maybe even dead, he'd be of no help to Meg Swope. Better that he play it smart.

67

Slowly Bart drew himself to his feet, every muscle and bone in his body throbbing with pain. He glanced at the girl. She was standing to one side, shoulders against a tree, hands behind her. Fear brightened her eyes, and she was poised like a frightened deer about to take flight.

"All right—I've had enough," Foraker said wearily, and watched the terror tighten Meg's features. "I sure can't lick you all, and I reckon that means I can't keep the girl for myself. If it's sharing you want, that's what you'll get—but it'll be on my terms."

★ 11 ★

"Your terms!" Gilley shouted, and laughed. "Where do you get off thinking you got any say-so about the little filly?"

Foraker casually reached down, retrieved the pistol that had fallen from its holster during the altercation, and shoved it back into the leather. He did it slowly, in an offhand manner, half-expecting a challenge from Gilley or one of the other outlaws, but none came.

"My terms," he repeated flatly, convinced that from a position of weakness—the odds being three, probably four to one—his one hope was to make a show of strength and determination. "I've been looking out for the girl—saving her for myself, I reckon you could say—and that gives me the right to say how and where—"

"The hell it does," Hobie Green broke in. "Me and Ben and John Willie'll do the deciding."

"Then you and me ain't done fighting," Foraker said, shaking his head.

"Oh, hell," Ben Gilley said, "let him have his way. Ain't going to change nothing anyway."

Bart nodded, relief running through him. He glanced at Meg. Her face was a pale oval in the firelight as she stood rigidly off to one side. She appeared stunned by what Foraker had said, could not believe the words he had spoken.

Bart swung his attention to Crockett. "You going to be in on this, too?"

Reno bobbed. "Sure—why not? I ain't about to miss out on something like this. Who—"

"Come on, come on," John Willie cut in impatiently. "Get this here little sashay started!"

Foraker again looked at the girl. She seemed to have lapsed into the same state of mind that he and Reno had found her after the massacre. It was just as well, he supposed, although it could pose a problem.

"You can draw straws—short one wins," he said then to the outlaws.

"Wins—meaning what?" Gilley demanded. "Way I see it we're all going to win."

"Right, but one of you'll get to be first—the man with the shortest straw. Second man will be whichever one of you has the next shortest—and so on. You all savvy?"

Gilley, mollified, said, "Yeh, we savvy. How about you?"

"Sure, I'll be drawing, too," Foraker said at once. "My right, ain't it?"

"Reckon so—but I'm telling you right now, you better not draw the short straw!"

Bart shrugged. "Depends on luck, but we'll settle that if and when it happens," he said, and crossing to the edge of the camp, took up the blanket Meg used. Nodding to her, he added, "Come on, girl."

"Wait just a damn minute there," Hobie Green shouted instantly. "Where the hell you think you're going?"

Gilley and John Willie Poe had come to quick attention also, and hands resting on the guns at their hips, were looking on suspiciously. Only Reno seemed not alarmed.

Foraker, outwardly cool but gripped by tension,

shrugged. "You don't expect me to fix her a bed here, do you? Only right the lady have a little privacy."

The outlaws relented slightly. Gilley said, "Where you taking her?"

"Little patch of grass a short ways from here—"

"How far's a short ways?" John Willie wanted to know.

"Maybe fifty feet—could be less. You gents go right ahead with drawing straws. When I get things ready, I'll come back."

Bart didn't wait for either objection or approval, but took Meg Swope by the arm and, with the blanket over a shoulder, started off into the darkness of the cloudy night. Immediately the girl began to resist.

"No," Foraker cautioned in a guarded whisper. "Don't fight me—just do what I tell you."

Meg's resistance slackened. She had shaken off the lethargy present earlier, was again herself, and for that Bart was grateful. Dazed by fear, mind numb, she wouldn't have understood what she had to do.

"I'm going to try to get you away from here—from them," he explained quietly as they moved deeper into the shadow-filled brush, "but I'll be needing your help."

She turned her strained features to him. "Then—then you're not going to make me do—"

"Said I'd get you safely to San Luis—still aim to do it," Foraker stated firmly. Glancing over his shoulder, he halted. A pale-orange halo of firelight marked the location of the camp—now a sufficient distance off in the brush. Turning, he led her into a small clearing.

"Expect this will be as good a place as any," he said, and clearing the ground of rocks and bits of branches, he spread the blanket.

"Sit down," he directed.

Meg frowned, edged reluctantly toward the wool

71

cover. Foraker nodded reassuringly. "Don't be scared—I won't let anything happen to you."

Without further hesitation the girl took her place on the blanket.

"Stay right where you are—and trust me," Foraker said, moving off toward the camp. "I'll be back in a few minutes."

Reaching the circle of firelight, he looked inquiringly about. "Got everything all set," he said, crossing over to the lower side of the camp where Reno Crockett lazily reclined. "Who's the lucky man?"

"Me," John Willie answered at once. "And I'm sure anxious to see my bride!"

Bart shook his head sadly. "What kind of luck did I have in the drawing?"

"You got the longest straw—means you'll be last," Gilley said, laughing. Then, motioning to Poe, he said, "Get going, Tex. I'm plumb anxious myself."

John Willie threw the cigarette he was smoking into the fire and glanced at Foraker. "How'll I find her?"

"Just you walk straight away from the camp, and you'll run right into her," Foraker replied, and as Poe hurried off into the brush, he faded back into the shadows behind Reno Crockett.

He delayed briefly, watched, and listened as Ben Gilley, Green, and Reno fell to discussing an incident in which they had been involved some years previous.

"Be back in a bit," Foraker said. "Want to take a look at my horse—scared he's coming up lame."

Gilley, concerned with something being said by Hobie Green, waved an offhand approval, and Bart, moving casually, stepped farther into the brush and started toward the horses picketed a short distance off to the right. As soon as he was beyond any possible sight or hearing of the camp, Foraker changed course and, pistol in hand, hurried to where he had left Meg. Drawing

72

near, he could hear John Willie talking in a firm, insistent voice.

Time was precious, and Bart Foraker wasted none of it listening. Silent as smoke, he slipped in behind the Texan, on his knees before the girl, and clubbed him senseless with the butt of his forty-five. Taking Meg's hand, he drew her quickly to her feet.

"You know where the horses are?"

The girl's face was chalk white, and she was trembling visibly. "Yes—yes—"

"Want you to circle around, get my horse and one for yourself. Have to do it fast—and quiet. If anybody at the camp hears you, it'll be all over for both of us. Understand?"

Meg nodded and, wheeling, hurried off into the night.

Foraker brought his attention to the senseless John Willie Poe, sprawled out on the blanket. Straightening the outlaw's inert form, Bart wrapped the wool cover about him and dragged him deeper into the brush encircling the clearing.

"Hey, there, John Willie, how you doing?" Hobie Green's voice startled Bart. He pivoted, gun again in hand.

"You needing any help?"

Foraker pulled his bandanna up over his mouth to muffle his voice. "Nope—doing fine—good—"

There was no response. Foraker tensed. He had not fooled Green. John Willie's Texas drawl had betrayed him. Poised, Bart waited in the darkness, hearing not only Hobie Green advancing cautiously toward the clearing but the soft thud of the horses being brought up by Meg from the opposite direction.

"John Willie?"

Green reached the edge of the clearing, paused, eyes on the blanket-covered figure in the shadows.

"That you?"

73

Foraker, only a stride away, brought his weapon down with full force—he could not afford an outcry or even a moan from the outlaw, for such would surely bring both Ben Gilley and Crockett on the run.

He caught Green as he sagged, and lifting him off the ground to eliminate any noise, he laid him alongside the unmoving Poe. Coming hurriedly about, Bart crossed to where Meg waited with the horses.

The girl was ready and went into the saddle with no help from him as he took the reins of the bay from her and swung aboard.

"Follow me close—but no noise," he said, and headed the gelding off into the cloud-shrouded night.

★ 12 ★

For the first half-mile they moved at a fast walk, and then, well clear of the camp, Foraker slackened the pace. If their luck was running good, Ben Gilley and Reno would still be unaware of what had taken place, their belief being that Green and the Texan were still with Meg.

"Starting to rain," she said from the darkness on his left. Meg was riding a fairly large horse, probably the one that belonged to John Willie as the stirrups were adjusted for a tall man. Her feet barely reached the loops in the leather. "It'll wash out our tracks."

"Help some," Foraker agreed, "but not much. Reno knows which way we're headed, and he can guess about where we'll be. But don't worry about that bunch. I'll not let them back us into a corner again."

Meg fell silent as the horses plodded on. The rain had increased from a slight sprinkle to a steady drizzle, and the air had turned cold and was filled with the sound of drops beating a tattoo on the leaves of the trees and bushes while thunder rolled and vivid flashes of lightning lighted up the black sky.

Halting once, Bart removed his brush jacket and persuaded the girl to put it on. She was already wet to the skin and chattering violently from a chill, but the jacket did help some.

As they continued on, it came to Foraker that they

were now without food, that he would have to find some means of providing for Meg and himself. The nearest settlement, he recalled, would be Las Vegas—perhaps a day and a half away—and while he had planned to avoid the town, it appeared now that unless he could come up with another source, it would be necessary to forgo that decision. But he'd wait, make up his mind as to what was best to do when the time came; there was little gained in worrying about crossing a river till you came to it.

The rain ceased an hour or so later, but they pressed on, Foraker believing it wise to put as much distance as possible between the outlaws and them before daylight. Meg slept most of those last hours, sitting slumped, head down, legs dangling, hands gripping the saddle horn, while her horse obediently trailed along behind Foraker's bay.

On several occasions Bart halted to listen for sounds that would indicate that Ben Gilley and the rest of the outlaws were on their trail—thanks to Reno Crockett's directions—but he failed to hear anything. If they were, he realized, it would be difficult to pick up any noise, for the wet ground would deaden the thud of the horses' hooves, and the men themselves, wet and worn, would likely be riding in silence. He would simply have to keep a sharp watch out for them, be on the alert and ready to react if they put in an unexpected appearance.

With the first signs of dawn, little more than a dull glare behind thick, dark clouds banked along the eastern horizon, Bart Foraker cut away from the trail. Meg needed rest, as did he, but he took no chances; and doubling back along the path they had come, he halted in a thick stand of brush and trees. From there he could watch the trail, and if the outlaws had followed, he would see them pass, and being behind them, he could strike out on a different course.

76

Meg dismounted with no help from him, and picketing the horses close by, she settled down on a bit of dry ground beneath one of the thickly needled junipers.

"Can't take a chance on a fire, even if we could scare up some wood that would burn," he said, putting an arm around the girl to warm her as much as possible.

"I don't mind," she replied. "It's not the first time I've been wet and cold. . . . Do you think they'll find us?"

There was no way of being certain, of course, but Foraker said, "No, don't figure they will. If they do catch up, we'll see them first—and that'll give us a big advantage."

An uncomfortable thought came to him. Not only must he be wary of the outlaws, but now it would be necessary to watch for Sheriff Eben Burke and his posse, as well as for roving bands of Indians. A wry grin split his mouth. Added to those problems, he and Meg both were wet, cold, and hungry, and he was dead broke.

But he reckoned he'd be able to manage for them somehow; he'd been down before, and while he'd never had the law snapping at his heels, he had come through all right. If he . . .

"That woman," Foraker heard Meg say, "the one they claimed you—you murdered. You said you didn't do it. Is that true? I have to know."

Meg had been listening when he and Reno Crockett had discussed the crimes he was being accused of, and later she overheard what was said about it when Gilley and his two friends took over their camp. The possibility of his being guilty no doubt alarmed and troubled her.

A thin thread of resentment stirred him. She should know better, he thought. Had he been the kind who would assault and then kill a woman, certainly she

77

wouldn't be sitting at his side at that moment, safe and sound.

"That's why that posse you keep watching for is after you, isn't it?"

He nodded. "That's why—and if they get their hands on me again, I'll wind up swinging from a tree limb."

Foraker felt the girl, crowded against him for warmth, tremble, but she said nothing, and he knew she was waiting for him to answer her question.

"No—wasn't me that did it."

Bart could almost feel the relief that passed through Meg.

"Then what makes them think it was you?" she continued.

Foraker, eyes on the trail visible through the dripping brush and trees, shrugged, glanced up at the sky. It was clearing. The rain was over, he reckoned, and they should have a fine day.

"I was there at her ranch. Was early in the morning, and I was hoping to work out a bite to eat. Things hadn't been going so good for me.

"The lady came to the door when I knocked, and then, after I told her what I wanted, she put me to chopping a pile of firewood. When I was finished, she called me in and fed me a good breakfast—steak, potatoes, hot biscuits with fresh butter and honey, along with all the coffee I wanted. When I had my fill and got ready to leave, she handed me a sack of grub—"

"Was she a pretty woman?"

Foraker said, "Yes, she sure was. Had sort of yellow hair and brown eyes, and—"

"Did she have a nice figure?"

He frowned, rubbed at the whiskers on his jaw. "Yeah, I've got to say she was a fine-looking woman, but what I remember most was how kind she was and how good she smelled."

78

"Smelled?" Meg repeated.

"I guess she'd been baking bread and doing some cooking, and it was like she was wearing a perfume."

"I see," the girl murmured.

"I rode out then, after she gave me the sack of grub—bread and sliced meat and some spiced pickles. The last I saw of her she was standing in the doorway of the kitchen. I kept going until about the middle of the afternoon, then pulled up at a creek, made myself some coffee, and ate a little of what she had put in the sack. Was setting there enjoying it when the posse rode up and the sheriff told me he was taking me in for murder. Said I'd raped and killed a rancher's wife, and there was no sense denying it because they'd followed the tracks of my horse from her house to where they found me.

"That wasn't hard to believe. It had rained the day before and the ground was sort of soft, making it easy to trail me. I told the sheriff—his name's Eben Burke—that I'd been there, but I hadn't touched the woman, that she was all right when I rode off. Of course, he wouldn't believe me and told his deputy, a man named Pete Worley, to put a rope around me so's I couldn't get loose, and then we all started back to this town where he had an office—a place called Red Bluff, in Nebraska.

"They threw me in an old building, seems some prisoner ahead of me burned down the regular jail, and I was to go on trial the next day. That's where I run into Reno. He was in there, too, waiting for a U.S. marshal to come get him, take him off to be hung.

"I wasn't about to wait around for the judge that was coming and let them string me up for something I didn't do, so I figured out a way to escape. Reno put in his oar about then, said if I didn't take him along, he'd set up a holler, so I counted him in. Had in mind to get to Mexico, stay there till things cooled off, then come back and try to clear my name."

"You have an idea who did kill that woman?" Meg asked.

"All I've got's a hunch. It seemed to me that the deputy, Worley, know a little too much about things to have never been there, like he claimed. I thought about it a lot, figured that if it was him he must've come along about the time I was leaving, done the killing, and then wiped out his own tracks so's mine would be the only ones leading from the place. I aim to jump Pete Worley, tell him all that, and see if I can't make him own up to doing it.

"But that's something that'll have to wait until everything's blown over—a couple of years at least. Right now the whole country's up in the air about it. The rancher is well-known, and folks all liked his wife." Foraker paused, looked down at the girl. "That straighten it all out for you?"

Meg's eyes were partly closed, and she appeared to be in deep thought. She made no reply, simply continued to stare at the clump of brush directly in front of her. It occurred then to Bart that she probably didn't believe him, that she had grown up among people who held the belief that the law was always right, could make no mistakes, and who swore by that time-worn axiom: "Where there's smoke, there's certain to be fire."

He shrugged off his thoughts, feeling a pang of regret. If that was the case, Meg would just have to go on believing he lied—but it changed nothing. For her sake he would continue to look after her—just as he would if she were one of his sisters—and he would get her safely to her uncle in Colorado, despite everything. It was the only decent thing a man could do, but once the job was done, he'd turn and make tracks for Mexico, praying all the time that his luck, insofar as Burke's posse was concerned, would hold.

"Expect we'd best move out," he said. "Sooner we

get to Las Vegas, the sooner we can rustle up something to eat." Just how he would accomplish that was still a question, but as he'd decided earlier, he'd climb that fence when he came to it.

Meg drew herself away from him and got to her feet with him. Crossing to her horse, she climbed unaided into the saddle, wedged her toes in the stirrups loops, and looked down at him.

"I don't know what you're thinking," he said, "but what I've told you is the gospel truth. Up to you whether you believe me or not."

He stepped up to the bay after that and swung onto the gelding's back. He hoped Meg did believe what he'd said, although he wasn't sure at the moment just why it was important. He reckoned it was simply because he disliked the idea of her looking upon him as a killer and a defiler of women as well as a liar, but then he hated for anyone to think that of him.

Cutting the bay about, Bart headed back to the trail. There'd been no sign that the outlaws had followed them; now he hoped they had decided it was not worthwhile and given up the idea. He would like to be sure of that, for he would now have his hands full watching out for Burke and the posse who could—or could not—still be searching for him and Reno Crockett, and being on the alert for Indians who, likewise, could or could not still be prowling the area.

Bart swore softly. It was the uncertainty of things, the not knowing, that really got to a man and set his nerves on edge, he realized as they rode on. He could not recall of ever being trapped in such a tight spot before—a situation where it seemed the odds were all against him. But he guessed he'd come through it all right as long as he kept his eyes open and his gun handy.

Near dark, a whisp of smoke took shape on the skyline to the north and a short distance east of the towering Sangre de Cristo Mountains. The girl took no notice of it, but later, after darkness had closed in and lights began to appear in the distance, she moved her horse up beside him.

"Is that Las Vegas—those lights ahead?"

He nodded. "That's it," he answered, and let it drop.

Was she planning to break away from him once there, take her chances on making it to San Luis on her own? he wondered. Or was it a question put forth from sheer relief at the possibility of food and dry clothing?

★ 13 ★

Las Vegas was active at that early-evening hour, and it appeared that every saloon along its main street was well-patronized and going full tilt. Music intermingled with shouts and laughter filled the cool air. As Bart, with Meg Swope beside him, pulled up beneath a large cottonwood at the edge of the settlement, the question again rose in his mind as to how he might obtain a bit of food for them.

They'd had nothing to eat but the tough, stringy meat of a jackrabbit that he had been able to kill and roast over a fire late that morning. Thus, continuing on to San Luis, still two or three days to the north was out of the question until he could somehow lay in a supply of trail grub.

Foraker knew he himself could get by—he'd gone hungry for several days many times in the past—but Meg Swope was different. Though she didn't complain, he knew that she needed food, actually appeared to be growing weak, and when he considered just when she'd last had a good meal, it was to be expected.

"We'll leave the horses here," he said, tying them to the tree, "and take a walk along the street, see what we can turn up."

"Aren't you scared somebody might recognize you?"

Meg had spoken but little to him throughout the day, and the question surprised him somewhat.

83

"Why? It make a difference to you?" he asked, voice tinged with sarcasm.

"Yes—it does," she replied.

Foraker felt a twinge of regret. His sharpness had been uncalled for, he realized, but the possibility that the girl intended to leave him and go on her own when they reached Las Vegas had lain in the back of his mind, disturbing him and turning him irritable. It never occurred to Foraker to just let Meg strike out on her own, if that was what she wanted; he realized only that the girl would be no match for the world she would be entering and that he had to see her safely through to her kinfolk in Colorado.

"Chance I'll have to take," he said, "but the odds will be with me. Aim to stay out of the light as much as possible."

"If you need to go into a store, or someplace, let me do it. Nobody will pay any attention to me."

Bart smiled. They had reached the first of the buildings that lined the street, and were stepping up onto one of the intermittent sections of board sidewalk.

"You've never been in a town like this, else you'd not say anything like that," he commented.

They came to a saloon. Noise poured from its open door and light was spilling out into the night. Stopping at the edge of the yellow flare, Foraker threw his glance into the structure. He could see the free lunch provided for the paying customers—sliced meat, bread, a jar of pickled eggs—at the end of the bar, but there were far too many persons in the place for him to risk showing himself, and of course, sending Meg in was out of the question.

"Can forget this place," he said, and taking the girl by the hand, hurriedly crossed the island of lamplight.

An alleyway lay next along the sidewalk, one that separated the saloon from its adjacent neighbor, a darkened

84

clothing store. It was followed by a butcher shop, a printer, and the offices of a doctor and lawyer, all of which were also dark. But beyond them was another saloon, smaller, and not so well patronized as the first.

"Could have some luck here," Bart said, explaining the free-lunch possibility. "If there's no big crowd—and maybe using my gun—I can fix us up at least with enough for one meal. You wait—"

He broke off, hearing the quick beat of someone running toward the lower end of the street where they had left the horses. Shading his eyes from the intervening glare of light coming from the saloon, he concentrated on the darkness around the cottonwood. He could see no one in that vicinity and reckoned it was just someone leaving the saloon in a hurry.

"Was about to say it wouldn't be smart to give me the slip while I'm inside—if you're thinking on that. This town's one of the toughest this side of the Missouri, and a girl like you—young and pretty—would find herself in bad trouble mighty fast."

"I'm not planning on running away," Meg said, her voice tight.

"Glad to hear that—sort of thought maybe you were. Point is we're not far from San Luis now, and if we can somehow scare us up some grub, we'll soon be on our way."

He had shifted his attention from the smaller saloon ahead to one directly opposite. It was a much larger concern and it appeared that its customers had gathered to view something on its far side, leaving the bar pretty well deserted. It could be their best bet.

"Let's cross over," he began, and froze as he felt the hard, round muzzle of a gun pressing against his spine.

"No, I reckon not, Mr. Foraker," a strange voice said.

Meg sprang back, alarmed by the unexpected interruption. Bart swore. There had been someone behind

85

them after all—someone who had come out of that first saloon, circled around apparently, and come in on Meg and him from one of the alleyways.

"You're wasting your time," he said. "I'm flat broke—"

"I ain't caring nothing about that," the voice in the dark said. "Just you keep your hands up—and turn around."

Bart complied, pivoting slowly. "Who the hell are you—and what makes you think my name's Foraker?"

"You're him, for damn sure," the man said, a slim, sharp-faced individual in leather pants and laced shirt. "Seen you in Red Bluff when they brought you in for killing that woman. . . . You know they've got a thousand-dollar reward out for bringing you in?"

"That's what you're after—"

"Right—sure is. The way I make my living, in fact, catching and bringing in owlhoots like you that the law's willing to pay hard cash for. Folks call me Travis."

"A bounty hunter," Foraker mumbled, and shrugged.

Travis had shifted his weapon as Bart turned, was now leveling the pistol—a heavy, well-worn, large-caliber gun—at Foraker's chest.

"Where's that pardner of your'n—the one that busted out with you?"

"I've got no pardner—"

"The hell you ain't! His name's Crockett. Got away when you did. Stole a horse."

"Him? Was with me for a spell, then we split up. I think he headed west."

Travis swore. "Was hoping I'd find him with you. Got a thousand on his head, too—dead or alive. Sure could've used—"

"Well, you've got me. What's next?" Foraker cut in.

"Pulling your iron—I reckon that's next," Travis said, reaching forward carefully and lifting Foraker's pistol from its holster. "Then we'll—"

At that moment Meg Swope, ignored by the bounty hunter, threw herself out of the shadows along the building near which she stood, into Travis' side. The bounty hunter cursed as he rocked to one side, struggled to maintain his balance. Foraker, seizing the opportunity provided by the girl, made a grab for the pistol Travis was holding, and succeeded.

The two men swayed back and forth in the half-dark as they struggled for possession of the weapon. The bounty hunter was wiry and strong, but Foraker's superior weight and strength began to make the difference. Travis gave way, muttering curses with every gasping breath. He went to his knees as Foraker bore heavily against him—and then there was a muffled explosion as the weapon contested for by both went off.

The bounty hunter jolted, began to crumple as the bullet smashed into his chest, scorching the buckskin shirt he was wearing and setting up an acrid smell. Bart stepped free as Travis sprawled out on the warped sidewalk, and snatching up his pistol, glanced hurriedly about. The gunshot could have been heard, but no one was appearing along the street. He guessed the report had gone unnoticed, and bending down, he took Travis by the feet and dragged him into the alleyway next to the small saloon he had considered visiting.

Leaving the body there, Foraker returned to the walk, found Meg crouched, recovering coins that had slipped from the bounty hunter's pockets. Rising, she handed them to him.

"Where he's gone he won't be needing any money," she said with a wry smile.

Foraker looked down at the coins—two gold eagles, three silver dollars, and some small change.

"You're right," he said, and taking the girl by the hand, wheeled and started back to their horses.

★ 14 ★

Being careful not to be seen as they crossed in front of the small saloon at the end of the street, Foraker and Meg Swope returned to their horses and mounted.

"Need to find us a general store that's open. Can buy some grub now," he said.

The girl shook her head. "Everything seems to be closed but the saloons—I guess it's because it's so late. But if we do, I'd better go in and do the buying. That bounty hunter knew you—there'll be others."

Bart agreed. "Like as not the law's put up wanted dodgers for Reno and me all over town. Best we get out of here soon as we can, too—somebody's sure to come across Travis' body pretty quick."

Swinging away from the main street, they rode down the dusty, trash-littered lane that ran behind the buildings on the west side. When they came to the end of the row, it was apparent that only the saloons, detectable by their lights and continuing noise, were prepared to do business.

"What about the other side?" Meg wanted to know.

"Be the same. Regular stores are all buttoned up for the night. In a town like this it don't pay for them to stay open."

"Why? Back home the stores usually don't close so early. Folks who work in the fields or at some job all day have to do their buying then."

"Big difference out here. Things get rough after dark, or maybe I best say wild. . . . I'm going to see what I can get in that saloon across the street—the Rainbow, the sign says—it's sort of off to itself. If we can't find a store where we can buy some grub, maybe I can talk the bartender into selling us some."

As they started to cross over, trouble of some sort erupted midway down the street. Shouts went up, and a dozen or more men and several women surged out of one of the saloons and formed a loose circle in the pool of light coming from the open doorway of the building.

"Fight," Foraker said, and hurried on. "Could be it'll draw some of the Rainbow's customers and make the odds better for us."

They had completed crossing, had drawn up in the shadow of a large tree that spread its branches over the saloon. Two men appeared in the Rainbow's entrance, stepped out onto the landing, and stared toward the disturbance. Elsewhere along the way more people had come into the open and were turning their attention to the fracas, but none seemed interested in getting any nearer, simply remained where they were.

After two or three minutes' distant observation, most wheeled and went back into the saloon they were patronizing to resume whatever activity they had been engaged in. The men on the landing of the Rainbow were no exception, both also coming about and disappearing into the building's smoky interior.

Foraker swung down off his horse and handed the reins to Meg. "I won't take long," he said, and started for the entrance to the saloon.

A sudden yell sounded down the street at about the point where the fight—now over—had taken place. Bart realized at once what it meant: someone had stumbled upon the body of Travis, the bounty hunter.

"Get the marshal—somebody's been killed!"

The shout rose above the racket in the street. The two men came out of the Rainbow again, this time not halting on the landing but joining others attracted by the call for the town's lawman and hurrying toward the scene.

Foraker hesitated, considered what his best move would be; what he had feared would happen, had happened. The dead bounty hunter had been found and the town would now come alive with men searching for the killer. He decided he might as well go ahead with what he had in mind—he'd have a few minutes' grace—and continuing on, entered the saloon.

Passing through the doorway, Bart pulled his hat lower over his eyes. Three men were sitting at one of the half-dozen tables in the back of the room playing cards, clearly not interested in whatever was going on in the street. Nearby the bartender was looking on. When he saw Foraker, he leisurely turned, made his way in behind the counter, and faced Bart.

"What'll it be?"

"Whiskey," Bart replied, and as the man reached for a glass and bottle, he helped himself to some of the meat and bread on the bar.

"What's all the foofaraw down the street?" he asked as the saloon man filled the glass. "Big crowd—lot of yelling."

The bartender shrugged. "Hell, who knows? Always something busting loose around here. . . . Be a quarter—unless you want another shot."

"Reckon this'll do," Foraker said. "Sure hope you don't mind me helping myself to your eating. I'm a mite hungry."

"What it's there for—but if you're looking for a regular meal, there's a restaurant a couple of doors down the street. Go around to the back and knock, and they'll let you in."

90

The bartender, about to turn and resume his place as onlooker at the card game, paused, studied Bart thoughtfully.

"Just thinking I'd maybe seen you in here before," he said.

"Expect you have," Bart answered readily. "Been in town a few times." What he said was only partly true; he had been through Las Vegas several times in the past, but usually spent his money at the larger, more opulent Palace Saloon. "Working for a rancher west of here. Sent me in to do some buying—there a general store around here where I could fill my list?"

"Expect you got in too late—ain't nothing open at this time of night that I know of," the bartender said, starting to move off again. "Could try old man Gunderson. He's got a place out the east road a ways. Might roust him out of bed."

"Obliged," Foraker said, adding more of the bread and sliced meat to that he already had, and turned for the door. "I'll be dropping by again."

The bartender murmured a response unintelligible to Bart and crossed again to the card game, which had continued without interruption. Foraker, reaching the doorway, stepped out onto the landing. The crowd down the street had become larger, he noted as he returned to where Meg awaited him. Handing her two slices of the somewhat stale bread and several pieces of meat, he swung up into the saddle.

"Best I could do. Ask about a store, said maybe—"

"Do you think he recognized you?" Meg broke in, an anxious note in her voice.

"Not sure. Took a good look at me, but didn't seem too interested. Said we could find a store out east of here a ways."

Meg, munching hungrily on the poor lunch, nodded,

91

and as he cut the bay about, she quickly turned in behind him.

GUNDERSON'S GENERAL STORE . . . The sign across the false front of the small building was easily legible in the pale moonlight as they rode into the wagon yard fronting it.

"Dark," Meg said, her voice betraying her disappointment. "I was hoping—"

"The bartender said it likely was closed but maybe we could rouse Gunderson," Bart said, slipping off the bay. "I'll see what I can do."

Crossing the hardpack, he climbed the half-dozen steps to the landing and moved up to the door. There a fairly large bulletin board affixed to the wall nearby brought him to a halt. Among the handwritten notices of sales, strayed livestock, and such was one of the wanted dodgers he suspected was posted around the town.

Issued by Sheriff Ebenezer Burke of Red Bluff, Nebraska, it gave a full description of both him and Reno Crockett, and declared a reward of one thousand dollars each would be paid for them, dead or alive.

To rouse Gunderson under such circumstances would be foolhardy. The storekeeper would undoubtedly recognize him immediately, and even if he did nothing at the time, would quickly get the law, and a posse, on his trail only minutes after he and Meg rode off. Dropping back to where the girl waited, he told her about the dodger.

"Looks like we either go without grub—or I bust into the place. Can't risk letting this Gunderson see me—"

"Can't we get by without food? We've got a little of the meat you got at that saloon left, and—"

"Not enough to get us through—and we might have to hole up somewhere along the way for a couple of days."

He was thinking about Eben Burke and his posse.

That the lawman was still conducting an intensive search for Reno Crockett and him was apparent. If he and Meg spotted riders in the long stretch of country that lay between Las Vegas and San Luis that looked to be the law party, he'd have no choice but to go into hiding until it was safe to continue. There was also the matter of roving parties of Apaches, and of Ben Gilley, Reno, and their friends. There was no real assurance that they were not still on their trail.

"Pull over there into the shadows at the corner of the building," he said, coming to a decision. "I'm getting in that store. I'm kind of new at this, but I expect I can handle it. If you see a light come on, it'll mean I've woke up Gunderson, and you get away from here fast."

"Where'll I go?"

Foraker glanced off into the night. "Trees over there to your left about a quarter of a mile—wait there for me." He hesitated. "If something goes haywire, and I don't show up—"

Foraker broke off. He couldn't let anything go wrong; such would mean leaving a fifteen-year-old girl to shift for herself in a town where even grown women found survival difficult.

"Just set tight," he said, and removing his spurs and hanging them on the saddle horn with his hat, returned to the store's landing.

Quiet, he tried the door on a long chance that it had been accidentally left unlocked. It was securely closed by a crossbar resting in iron brackets. Moving along the wall, he tried the first window. It also failed to budge, but the one midway along the south side of the building gave an inch or so when he attempted to raise it.

Foraker needed no more; using his pistol, he wedged the barrel under the partly open sash and applied leverage. The window resisted briefly, and then, as the peg preventing its movement broke and came free, Bart was able to raise it enough to permit his entering the building.

Inside, Foraker quickly lowered the pane. The dry wood in its channel squeaked some as he returned it to its normal position, and he had a quick fear the sound might attract Gunderson. Crouched in the semidarkness between a counter and the wall, he waited out a full five minutes, and then, when there was no sign of the storekeeper or anyone else in the building having been disturbed, Bart rose, and locating a flour sack on a shelf nearby, he hurriedly began to go through the grocery stock, choosing food that could be easily prepared while on the trail.

Filling the sack fairly well, Foraker added a coffeepot, a couple of tin plates, cups, eating utensils, and a frying pan. That brought to mind a personal need, and looking about, he located a glass-fronted case wherein were displayed sheathed skinning knives. Selecting one, he thrust it under his belt; he'd take time later to slide the leather strip through the slots.

Pausing after that, he searched his mind for anything needed that he might be overlooking. The faint creak of a door opening slightly sent a warning through him. Instantly he dropped to a crouch behind the counter where he had found the display of knives. The door creaked again, and he realized it was being opened wider. Drawing his pistol, Bart waited. If it became necessary, he'd use the weapon to knock out the storekeeper, or whoever it was; he'd not shoot unless forced to.

Once more the door creaked, and then a voice broke the tense hush.

"Nothing—it was nothing."

A woman immediately replied. "Something it was, Levi! I heard!"

"Mice probably. A cat I will see about getting tomorrow. Let's get back to bed."

Foraker waited until he heard the door close and then, rising, dug into his pocket for one of the gold eagles that had fallen from the bounty hunter's pocket. Laying it on the counter where it would be found by Gunderson when he opened for business that next morning, Bart returned to the window, carefully raised it, and lowering first the sack of groceries and other items to the ground, let himself out and hurriedly rejoined Meg Swope.

★ 15 ★

"I—I was beginning to worry," Meg said, her voice reflecting the strain she was feeling.

"Gunderson and his wife came in—had heard me," Foraker said, hanging the sack on the saddle horn after reclaiming his hat and spurs.

"They didn't see you?"

"No—I kept out of sight, and they didn't look very hard," he replied, mounting. "Best we get out of here, though."

Far back in his mind as he cut the bay around, a thread of concern had begun to build; the bartender at the rainbow—he couldn't shake the recollection of how the man had so carefully studied him and then the apparent disinterest. And with those wanted posters being around . . .

Foraker headed back along the road they had taken out of the settlement, but when they reached a point where there were no houses, he veered off and took a diagonal course for the trail that led northward. By so doing they could avoid town and any activity that might be in progress at that hour.

Suddenly they heard the quick pounding of running horses. Bart swerved again, this time in behind a thick stand of feathery tamarisk someone in previous years had planted as a windbreak. Meg was only a breath behind him, and well hidden, they watched four riders rush by on the road east.

"Gunderson's place!" a voice shouted above the drumming of the horses. "Holcomb said he sent him to Gunderson's!"

"Gunderson's!" another voice called back in confirmation, and said more, but the words were lost in the sound of the running horses.

He'd been right about the Rainbow bartender, Foraker thought. The man—Holcomb, apparently—had recognized him, and in hopes of collecting the thousand-dollar reward, or a good portion of it, had got together a posse and sent it out to the Gunderson store. He and Meg had left the place just in time.

"Let's move out," he said in a quick sort of way, and putting the bay into motion, continued a slanting course for the north road.

When they reached the end of the town's main street, now some distance to their left, Foraker threw his glance along its length. Drifting dust shot with lamplight from the saloons still hung in the canyonlike area between the two rows of buildings, evidence of the posse's rapid passage.

There was no crowd now down where the bounty hunter's body had been found, but there were several men standing about in conversation. There was no way of knowing what the subject might be, of course, but Bart reckoned it had to do with Travis' death and the fact that he had been seen in the settlement. No doubt he'd get credit for the man's death, which, he had to admit, was only right.

They pressed on, now following a hilly road that led on to Colorado. Weariness was catching up with Meg, he saw when he turned to have a last, precautionary look at the settlement; he knew it would be necessary to halt before long and make camp. He, too, was feeling the need for a good meal and rest, but they both would have to wait until they were a fair distance from Las Vegas. He could afford to take no chances; San Luis was now too close to gamble on failure.

Foraker kept the horses at a slow lope for an hour and then pulled them down to a fast walk for an equal length of time. By then Meg Swope was all but falling off the saddle from exhaustion, and watching until they were abreast a stand of trees and brush a distance off the trail, Bart cut off and led the way to where they halted.

He helped the girl from her mount and to a place where grass offered a fairly comfortable bed, and there left her while he saw to the horses. He watered the animals with a bit of water poured from the canteen into his hat, and then he picketed the pair a bit farther back in the grove where they could not possibly be seen or heard by anyone on the road.

Returning to where he had left Meg, bringing with him the sack of grub and canteen, he debated the idea of awakening her and preparing a meal of sorts. He decided against it. The bit of food he'd acquired at the Rainbow saloon's free lunch counter and given to Meg had dulled her hunger just as what he'd eaten had tempered his need; it would be better for them both to sleep and prepare for themselves a good meal in the morning.

Hanging the grub sack from a limb of a nearby tree where it would be safe from the small animals that inhabited such areas, Foraker chose a spot on the grass not far from Meg and stretched out. He wished now he'd picked up a couple of blankets while he was in Gunderson's, but the unexpected arrival of the storekeeper and his wife had caused him to overlook the need—just as he'd neglected to get a jacket or coat for the girl to wear so he might reclaim his own from her. But in the unfamiliar role of burglar, he could not be expected to think of everything, he supposed.

He had barely closed his eyes, it seemed, when he felt the first warm rays of the sun on his face. Sitting up hastily, he glanced about. It was well past daybreak, he saw. Rising, he started across the small grassy hollow where they had halted to rouse Meg, slowed when he saw that she was already awake.

"I would've fixed something to eat," she said, also coming to her feet, "but I wasn't sure if I should build a fire or not."

Bart looked off into the direction of Las Vegas and the road coming from it. "Expect we need something hot, so we'll take a chance. While I scare up some dry wood that won't smoke much, you see what you can come up with from the grub sack. Need coffee for sure."

Meg nodded, frowned. "Water—what'll I do for water? There's no spring—"

"Use what you need out of the canteen. We'll be crossing some streams today and can fill up then."

Foraker moved off into the grove and began to collect dead branches and twigs that were beneath the brush and at the base of the trees. When he had an armload, he returned to camp, found the girl had laid out the side of bacon he'd obtained at Gunderson's, along with potatoes, onions, bread, and canned peaches. Handing her his new skinning knife to work with, he set about building a fire pit, got a quantity of wood in it to blazing, and then, not leaving it up to the girl, poured a sufficiency of water into the coffeepot and set it to boil.

"I was thinking," he heard Meg say as he turned away, "There's no need for us to go on to San Luis."

He came about, stared at her in surprise. "What do you mean?"

"I want to go with you to Mexico," she said, simple and straightforward.

99

Foraker let that ride for a few moments, and then, "I reckon you're just talking—"

"No—I don't care a hoot about going to live with my uncle and his family. I don't even know them—only about them—and being with you these last days, I've realized what it is I really want."

"Best you—"

"No—wait, let me finish. I want to be with you, Bart. It doesn't matter that you're on the run and having to hide from the law—or even if you never clear your name of that murder charge—I only know that all that matters is us, you and me—me being your wife."

He shook his head as he watched her. All the time she was talking Meg had continued to work at preparing the meal, as if she needed to keep busy while she spoke.

"Meg, I'm not sure you—"

She paused at that and looked up at him. "You don't already have a wife, do you?"

"No," Bart said, and saw the planes of her face smooth with relief. "It just wouldn't be right."

"Would for me. I can cook, sew, keep a good house if we ever wanted one. And I'd look after you, take care of you no matter what or where—"

"Meg," Foraker cut in firmly, "listen to me. You'd make a fine wife, and I'd be real proud to have you for mine, except for one thing—"

"One thing?" she prompted when he paused.

"You're too young to start being a wife."

"Young!" she echoed, placing the skillet with its strips of bacon over the fire. "I'm fifteen! Why, I know some girls back home who married at twelve and thirteen! And I'm big for my age and filled out better than a lot of older women I've seen."

Foraker, hunched on his heels, shook his head. "I'm not denying anything you say, but you're still too young, and I'll not rob you of your growing-up years. You'll

100

find being a wife in this country is mighty hard on a woman—turns her old way before her time—and I sure won't be a party to letting that happen to you."

Meg was silent as she added a handful of ground coffee to the water now simmering in the pot. "Would you want me for your wife if I was older?" she asked.

Bart nodded. "I would," he said, rising from his squatting position. "Expect I'd better see to the horses."

Moving quickly off into the grove, he made his way to the animals, glad to leave the girl for a few minutes. He would like nothing better, he realized, now that he permitted himself to think of it, then to have Meg Swope for his wife. Even in the brief period of time they had been thrown together, she had done something to him—had made him not only face up to the pointless kind of life he was leading, but also come to terms with the future.

But he just couldn't feel right about making her his wife. If she were a couple of years older, he wouldn't hold back for a moment—but only fifteen . . . it was out of the question.

The bay and the mouse-colored dun, or grulla, that Meg was riding had fared well, and tightening the cinches and slipping the bits into place, Foraker prepared them for the day's traveling. It was when he was completing that chore that he heard the rapid beat of approaching horses. Alarm lifting within him, he crossed to an opening in the brush and put his attention on the road.

Seven riders. . . . Studying them intently, he recognized Reno Crockett's three friends—Ben Gilley, Hobie Green, and the Texan John Willie Poe. The remaining four, he decided after a time, were the men who had ridden out to Gunderson's in search of him. Apparently Reno's friends had thrown in with the quartet later, and now all were out to get the reward offered for him.

Crockett was not in the party. Did that mean his onetime partners had double-crossed him, turned him over to the law in Las Vegas when they learned of the price being offered for him—or had Reno simply split from Gilley and the others and was on his way to Mexico?

★ 16 ★

Meg watched Bart Foraker stride off into the cool morning haze toward the horses, and then, taking up an onion, began to slice it into the spider, sizzling busily with its other contents.

She couldn't understand Foraker. She was certain that he wanted her, really loved her, in fact—she had lived around men enough to recognize such in the way he looked at her—yet he insisted she was too young to become a wife.

Shoot! Back home in North Carolina it was no big thing for a girl of twelve to get married—girls not half as smart or near as grown as she was. And what made it all the more confusing, she'd always understood that men wanted young wives—but Bart Foraker, he seemed to look at it like it was some kind of a sin!

Meg trembled a little at the thought of becoming his wife—not with fear but from a delicious sort of excitement and happiness. That she could make him a good wife was certain; schooled at home by her women kinfolk in cooking, sewing, housework, as well as yard chores, she knew she lacked nothing along those lines.

And she reckoned she was as pretty as the next girl, actually prettier than most. A lot of her girlfriends back home, some even older than her, had not filled out, womanwise, as she had—but were actually skinny as a rail.

That Bart appreciated all that was evident, and that he wanted her as much as she wanted him was also plain. What he needed, she supposed, was a shove—like when she and some of her girlfriends went swimming down in the pond near Wagon Road Gap, there was always a couple who needed a push to get them into the water because they were leery of getting wet.

Abandoning the frying pan for the moment, Meg set the pot of coffee off to one side and, reaching for the loaf of circular bread, hacked off two large chunks with the hunting knife Foraker had given her to use.

She must come up with an idea that would cause Bart to change his thinking—and do it soon. She recalled his saying they were not far from San Luis—only a couple of days, in fact—but if she handled things right, sort of pushed herself onto him, made him see that he really needed her, maybe she could win out over this foolish idea he had about her being too young to be his wife.

Or woman . . . It could be that was the catch—the real reason. Perhaps he just didn't want to tie himself down with marriage vows—a lot of men were that way, she knew—but he'd not object to her becoming his woman.

Meg, having placed the chunks of bread at the edge of the fire to warm, began stirring the contents of the frying pan once more. The mixture was ready, she saw, and setting it aside, she took up the tin plates and prepared to serve.

A sort of contentment had settled over her now that she'd thrashed out in her mind the problem she had with Bart Foraker. She knew what had to be done now, and hearing the sound of his steps as he returned, she looked up smilingly, prepared to take the first necessary steps.

"Posse went by—heading north," Foraker said in a

104

clipped sort of way as he settled down to eat. "Was those outlaw friends of Reno's and the four men that bartender at the Rainbow sent after us last night."

Meg, frowning, considered his words. "North—that means they'll be ahead of us."

Bart, pouring himself a second cup of coffee after hurriedly finishing his plate of breakfast, shook his head. "Maybe, but I doubt if they'll go far. Posses like that one ain't known for ever working hard. Expect they'll be doubling back for Las Vegas when they don't catch sight of us pretty soon."

"Are we staying here?"

"No, don't think we ought to do that. I figure to cut back toward the mountains, keep in the trees and brush. That'll put a mile or so between us and the trail. Good chance they'll never spot us when they come back this way."

"Wasn't Reno with them?" Meg asked, beginning to scrape the leavings on the dishes into the fire.

"No. Expect he's either in jail or on his way to Mexico. . . . I'll bring up the horses."

The girl nodded, and her cleaning chores done, began to store the pans and dishes and the remainder of their food stock in the grub sack. Foraker, in better spirits after the night's rest and the good meal, was eager to resume the journey to Colorado, and San Luis. Once there, and Meg handed over to her kin, he could turn and start again for Mexico—alone now. He'd sort of miss Meg, he realized; she was good to have around, and although they had been together but a short time, it would seem strange when the girl was gone.

Girl . . . That brought to mind her offer to go to Mexico with him, become his wife. He had tried to make her understand that it would suit him fine, only she was just too young for such. And in addition to that, he simply had nothing to give her in the way of a decent life.

There would first be the problem of getting to Mexico, which was becoming more difficult with each passing day as word calling for his arrest—bolstered by a fat dead-or-alive reward—spread throughout that part of the country. And if he managed to reach the border with her, he would be faced with the uncertainties of staying alive in a hostile land where he had no friends or acquaintances. It would be a starve-out, hand-to-mouth existence at best, and if . . .

Foraker, in the act of leading the horses back to the camp, came to a stop. A deep frown creased his forehead. Off to the right, in the direction of the trail, he had heard the distinct click of a horse's iron shoe striking rock.

Holding the lines of the bay and the grulla, Bart crossed quickly to the edge of the trees, and keeping a screen of brush before him, glanced toward the road. The frown on his forehead deepened.

The posse, with Ben Gilley and one of the men sent out to Gunderson's by Holcomb, the bartender at the Rainbow, was coming toward the grove. Evidently, after passing on by, they had decided to double back and have a look in the stand of trees, thinking it just might be the place where he and Meg Swope would set up camp.

Delaying no longer, Foraker led the horses to where the girl was waiting. She had everything ready, he saw with satisfaction, and halting beside her, took up the grub sack and hung it from the horn of his saddle.

"What is it—what's wrong?" she asked, seeing the hurried tenseness of his manner.

"That posse—they've turned back. They're headed for here."

Meg's features tightened. "But how could they know we'd be here?"

He glanced at her. She had found time to freshen her appearance; using a bit of water from the canteen to wet a handkerchief, he supposed, Meg had wiped her face and then had drawn her dark hair into a bun on the back of her neck. The blueness of her eyes had brightened with concern at word of the posse's nearness, and her well-shaped lips were compressed into as straight a line as their fullness would permit.

"They don't, leastwise not yet," Foraker said. "I expect somebody had a hunch. . . . Get mounted."

Meg turned at once and went into her saddle. Earlier Bart had taken time to shorten the stirrups, and now she was able to seat herself comfortably and ride with more security.

"Head straight for the mountains," Foraker said, swinging up onto the bay. "We'll find plenty of cover there."

The sounds of the approaching posse, considerably muted by the trees, were still audible as Meg and Foraker rode out of the small clearing where they had spent the night. He was careful to follow none of the traillike aisles in the trees and brush, but kept to a course that allowed them to remain well in the growth.

"Was right!" a voice sang out behind them. "Camped right just like I figured—and they ain't been gone long! Ashes are still plenty warm."

Foraker couldn't recognize the voice, guessed it was one of the four that had ridden to the Gunderson place looking for him.

"Which way you reckon they went?"

"They sure didn't head north or south. Or east, either, or we'd have seen them—"

"Means they've took off for the mountains—"

Foraker, urging the bay and Meg's mount to a faster

107

pace, looked ahead. They were breaking out of the grove and starting up the slope of a foothill—one that offered but little cover for the first hundred feet or so. Beyond that lay the mountain proper, and its growth of pines, piñons, and scrub brush and its large boulders—all of which offered ample protection. As soon as . . .

"There they go!" a voice suddenly yelled. "They're heading up the side of the mountain!"

★ 17 ★

A gunshot blasted the stillness of the hills, sent up a rolling chain of echoes. Meg screamed in fright as the bullet struck a rock just beyond her, sending up a shower of splintery particles as it went shrilling off into space.

"Keep low!" Foraker shouted, swinging the bay in behind her. Slapping the grulla sharply on the rump and sending him surging forward, he added, "Make for that big boulder straight on!"

As both mounts lowered their heads and dug into the loose soil with their hooves as they struggled to climb, Bart drew his weapon and threw an answering shot at the posse. He could see none of them, could only guess where they might be.

Almost at once the horses began to labor on the stiff grade. Patches of sweat darkened their hides and foam gathered about their muzzles. Twice the bay went to his knees, only to regain his footing and struggle on. It would be necessary very soon to let them break from the uphill pull and strike a course across the side of the slope, or else halt completely.

More gunshots sounded above the rattle of sliding gravel and the thudding of hooves below. Again there was the sharp striking of bullets as they drove into tree trunks or screamed off rocks. Dust was now hanging on the side of the mountain in a blanketlike reddish pall, and Bart realized that serving as a curtain, it was preventing the posse members from getting a view of him and Meg.

Meg! Anger whipped through Bart Foraker. The posse was shooting wildly, making no effort to not hit the girl, hoping only that one of their bullets would bring him down. That they might hit, or even kill, Meg—an innocent party in the chase—was not being considered by them. Twisting about, hanging on to the saddle horn with one hand to prevent being thrown from the plunging, straining horse, Bart triggered two more shots in the general direction of their pursuers.

The boulder he'd indicated to Meg was now but a few yards farther up. It rested on a sort of ledge, a huge gray irregular mass of granite behind which he felt certain they could find shelter long enough for the horses to recover wind and strength.

Meg's mount went down, but like the bay, was back up in an instant and climbing on. The girl drew abreast the boulder, veered in behind it, and halted. Foraker followed only moments later.

Both horses, heads swung low, sides heaving, were ready to cave in. Bart, slipping off the saddle, hurried around the rock for a look downslope. He could see movement through the smoky dust in the trees, and quickly reloading his pistol, sent three bullets into the area. Motion halted at that, and he reckoned he'd been lucky, winged one of the men, and driven the others to seek safety from his marksmanship behind some of the trees—but they would not remain so for long. Pivoting, he hurried back to Meg.

"Can't stay here," he said, taking the bay's reins and going into the saddle. "Best bet's to try and lose them."

Cutting the bay around, Bart started across the face of the slope, bearing northward. The going was slow, and as there was no trail, not even one used by deer and

110

other animals, the horses continually slipped as loose rock and dirt slid out from under their weight and rattled noisily down the grade.

They would never lose the posse this way, Foraker realized. The sounds of their passage could be heard for a considerable distance—and certainly by Gilley and the men with him, who were only a hundred yards or so away.

Meg was having trouble staying in the saddle as her horse fought to keep his footing on the unstable surface. Twice, as Bart watched, she was almost thrown, and it became clear to Bart that he would have to change course again, try to find a smoother route.

He glanced off into the direction of the posse. A heavy pall was continuing to hang over the slope, but he could detect blurred movement through it. The riders were climbing, were endeavoring to climb to the level he and Meg were on, and soon they would be above the screen of yellow dust. The result of their accomplishing that was clear; he and the girl must either drop back down—which could mean running into some of the men riding across the lower part of the mountain—or they would have to chance going higher.

Bart doubted the horses could stand much more of the stiff uphill climb at a pace that would be necessary to keep them beyond the reach of the outlaw's view—and guns. But he must do something . . . and quick; the sounds of the horses coming up the grade, the shouting of the men, were growing louder.

Directly ahead he saw a darkness on the face of the slope. It was beyond a heavy rock slide and appeared from where they were to be either a deep overhang on the mountainside or a cave.

"Head for that," he called to Meg as he pointed.

The girl, features taut, nodded, and drumming the side of the grulla with her heels, urged him on.

111

It proved to be the latter, and showed signs of having been used by various wild animals. "Want you to ride in there, and wait," Foraker directed as he swung off his horse.

Both mounts were reluctant to enter, not liking the smell of bear and mountain lion, which were apparently the most recent tenants, but working together, Meg and Foraker finally got them inside.

"Where—where are you going?" Meg asked worriedly, her voice faltering.

"Got to draw that bunch off," he replied, reloading his weapon as he dropped back to the entrance to the cave.

"Wouldn't it be better if you took your horse—rode?"

"No. He'd be more trouble than he'd be worth. Footings too loose, and they'd hear me coming. He needs the rest anyway. Soon as I'm back we'll light out—for the north."

Ducking low, Bart left the mouth of the shallow inset, and at as good a run as he could manage, started up the slope, intending to get above the posse. Once there, he'd open fire on them to draw their attention, lead them off into the opposite direction, and thereby keep them away from the cave.

Abruptly a rider broke into view a dozen yards away. It was John Willie Poe. The Texan, as surprised as was Foraker, hauled back on the reins and brought his horse to a precarious halt.

"Over here!" Poe yelled, grabbing for his pistol. "They're over here!"

Breathing hard for wind, Bart leveled a hurried shot at the man and went down as loose rock and gravel went out from under him. Poe, apparently hit but not seriously, yelled again, fired his weapon, and then fought to keep his horse from heading back down the steep slope.

Foraker, scrambling to his feet, rushed on, recklessly plowing ahead across the face of the mountainside while he maintained a sharp lookout for the rest of the posse members. He still wasn't far enough away from Meg to circle back, figured he'd need to go at least another hundred yards or so—and then, only if he could manage to keep Gilley and the others working into the opposite direction . . .

Suddenly Ben Gilley was before him. The outlaw's head came back. An oath ripped from his lips and he brought up his gun. Foraker, weapon already out and in hand, drove a bullet into Gilley before the outlaw could get off his shot. Ben yelled, fell backward off the saddle of his nervously shying horse, struck the ground, and began to roll and slide down the grade.

"Up there—above us," a voice shouted. "He's gone and shot Ben! Somebody head him off on the left!"

Foraker, badly winded, endeavoring to run, now and then clawing for a hold on the scraggly brush growing on the slope, saw a second man appear. It was one of the four Holcomb had sent to get him. Dropping prone, Bart leveled a careful shot. He saw the man grab at his shoulder, heard him yell, and then watched him turn his horse about and start down the grade.

More shouts went up, and now making as much racket as possible, Bart continued on across the slope—not pausing to do so, but kicking loose the smaller rocks and firing at various intervals to establish in the minds of the posse the direction he was moving.

Shots broke out once more a few minutes later. He felt the sear of a bullet as it raced across his forearm, hesitated long enough to pinch out the smoldering fire it started in his sleeve, and plunged on. A hard grin split his mouth. That one was close—too close! He'd best start being a bit more careful, not be so ready to expose himself.

He reached a small, level area behind several fairly large boulders that had apparently rolled down from a higher level on the mountain during one of the wild rainstorms that periodically lashed the rugged formation, and he dropped to his knees. Breathing hard, he swiped at the sweat on his forehead, hurriedly reloaded his pistol, and then crawled to where he had a view of the slope below.

A grunt of satisfaction slipped from his throat. The posse was making its way across the mountainside some hundred yards or so farther down. He counted five riders, reckoned he had put two of them out of the hunt—Ben Gilley for good.

He lay motionless for a good quarter-hour behind the rocks, watching the riders gradually work farther to the south; then, he rose, and in hopes of keeping them believing he was still ahead and above them, chose an apple-size rock and hurled it as far as he could in the direction of, but above, the posse.

Turning then, Foraker headed at a run for the cave where he had left Meg Swope and the horses.

★ 18 ★

Meg was anxiously awaiting him, and when he appeared from behind a ridge of weedy soil and rocks, a glad smile parted her lips and she ran to meet him.

"You're all right," she cried, throwing her arms about him. "I heard all that shooting, and—" Abruptly the girl broke off, seeing the bloody smear on his arm.

"You've been shot," she said, drawing back.

"Scratch, nothing more," he said. "Let's get out of here. The posse's heading south, but they'll soon decide they're on a snipe hunt and start back this way."

Meg had turned to her horse and was leading him into the open. Just beyond her on a jutting bit of rock, a striped chipmunk was looking on in bright-eyed curiosity.

"I almost went out to look for you," she said as she climbed into her saddle. "All those gunshots—I thought maybe you were lying out there on the slope hurt, bleeding and needing me."

Foraker, on the bay, studied the girl for a long breath. It had been a long time since anyone had cared whether he lived or died.

"Appreciate your thinking about me," he said softly, "but at times like that it's best to look at it this way—I'll be back or I won't. If you had come, you would've just made it harder on yourself. . . . Ready?"

She nodded, somewhat crestfallen at the faint rebuke,

115

and followed him away from the cave. They began a slow, gradual descent, and when they reached the comparative level ground at the base of the mountain, they went on among the low, skirting junipers, mahogany, and other growth that formed a band at that level. Foraker had resumed their northward course, and as they worked steadily along, they neither saw nor heard any signs of pursuit on the part of the posse and assumed the men were still searching for him well to the south.

Traveling was slow at first, but as they drew farther from the scene of the encounter and low hills and dense growth began to close in behind them, Foraker deemed it safe to work out more onto the flat paralleling the towering hills; there the horses would find more comfortable footing.

Late in the morning, with still no signs of the Las Vegas posse, Bart sighted a lone rider well to the east pointing also for Colorado.

He kept a close eye on the man and horse for over an hour as they rode steadily on. There was a possibility that the horseman could be one of Sheriff Eben Burke's deputies sent out to scour that part of the country for him and Reno Crockett. The area was one where the lawman likely would concentrate his search, being not only on a natural line for Mexico from the Nebraska settlement, but one known also to have a scarcity of lawmen.

But the solitary rider made no stops and appeared to have no particular interests other than reaching whatever destination to the north he had in mind, and after a time Bart dismissed him from his thoughts.

They halted at noon in a grove west of an army fort, ate a cold lunch while the horses rested for an hour, and then again mounted and were on their way.

Foraker saw no more of the lone rider as he resumed

116

his constant watch for Burke and his posse, Indians, and the men from Las Vegas, and when the day began to end with a fiery display of color in the sky beyond the Sangre de Cristos, he felt it safe to stop along a narrow, willow-bound creek and make camp.

Again taking precautions, he built a small, near-smokeless fire for Meg to use in preparing a hot meal, and then set about caring for the horses. They'd had a long, hard day, first as they climbed the mountain, later struggling to keep their footing as they labored across it, and then, once off the treacherous grade, the long hours of steady going as they moved north.

In the fading light Foraker loosened the saddle cinches, slipped the bridles so that the animals would be free of the iron bit when they grazed, and then examined the hooves of both. The bay's appeared little worse for the time on the mountain, but Meg's horse was in need of shoes; all four were badly worn, and one was slightly loose.

Bart corrected that as well as he could by using a rock for a hammer; the shoe would have to last until they got to where there was a blacksmith—and that meant San Luis. Once there, it wouldn't matter, for Meg would be home—with her uncle and his family—and the matter of a worn, loose shoe would be of no consequence.

When he had finished with the horses, Bart returned to Meg, found that she had the meal ready. They ate in silence, the girl curiously so, and not long after they had finished, he sought out a comfortable place to sleep.

"This ought to be the last night you'll have to spend in the open," Foraker said, taking note of the girl's depressed manner. "Should get to your uncle's place by this time tomorrow, if we don't run into trouble."

Meg gave that thought. Then, "Trouble? You mean from those men back on the mountain?"

"No, expect we've shook them, but we're up where

we're liable to run into that bunch looking for Reno and me—Sheriff Burke's posse."

"But you haven't seen any sign of them today, have you?"

"No. Was one rider way off there to the east. Thought he might be one of Burke's scouts, but I guess he wasn't."

"Then, if there's been no reason to think this Burke's around somewhere, why are you fretting about him? Would seem to me he's somewhere else."

"Maybe. It's not knowing for sure about something that keeps you looking. If I knew where he was, I'd figure how to keep plenty clear of him and his men and not be wondering if I was going to bump into him accidentallike."

Meg thought over his logic for a minute or two and finally shrugged. Lying back, she curled up near the fire, leaving Foraker to wonder if she understood or not.

Still and cold, they were up early next morning, warmed themselves by a fire, and after eating a hasty breakfast—again bacon, greased-soaked fried bread, and strong, black coffee—they packed up and were on their way.

Around midmorning they sighted a band of Indians to the northeast and halted in a stand of brush while Bart gave them close observation.

"Are they the Apaches again—that same bunch, I mean?" Meg asked.

Foraker shook his head. "Can't tell from here, but I expect they're Arapaho. Apaches are not likely to be up this far. Looks sort of like it's a small village on the move—women, kids, dogs, the works."

Bart and the girl moved and a time later spotted another lone rider, this one going south in the direction of Las Vegas.

It was while they were halted at noon that Foraker

118

saw Eben Burke and his posse. The lawman, with the sun glinting off his star as it did off several of the deputies accompanying him, appeared abruptly a short distance to the east of where he and Meg had stopped.

The men had been following out a deep arroyo, Bart reckoned, else they would have seen him—or he them—earlier. The wash had petered out and brought them to the level of the plain, which accounted for their sudden presence.

Fortunately Bart Foraker had built no fire and had, without conscious thought, chosen a spot well back in the brush to rest and have lunch. He and the girl watched in silence as Burke and his men pressed steadily on, taking a course that would lead them into Colorado.

"Could be the sheriff's calling it quits," Foraker said hopefully. "If he starts bending to the east after a bit, it'll mean he's going back to Nebraska. That's where he started from."

Meg shook her head. "Looks now like he's riding straight for Colorado. Seems that's where everybody's going."

"Road he's following cuts across a corner of Colorado. If he stays on it, he'll wind up in Nebraska—like I said."

They watched the posse until it dropped from sight an hour or so later, and then once more they resumed their journey. The sky-piercing peaks of the Colorado mountains were now much nearer, and despite the warm August sun, there was a crispness in the air.

"Bart—"

At Meg's voice Foraker turned to her. They were riding side by side across a vast swale, green with grass and bright with red and pink bee plants and the vivid blue of wild flax.

"Yeh?"

"Have you thought any more about taking me with you to Mexico?"

119

He stirred on his saddle. "Figured we'd settled that."

"I suppose we did, but I can't help hoping. I—I don't want to go and live with my uncle and his family; I want to go with you."

Again he shrugged. As before, he agreed with himself that having Meg for a wife would be a fine thing, except for the fact that she was much too young, and such would lie on his conscience like a deadweight.

How would he feel about it, he asked himself, if Meg were one of his sisters and at that same tender age was about to marry a man in his position—wanted by the law, broke, and on the run to Mexico, where he would live a precarious existence with only a slight hope of one day clearing his name? He'd never agree to it, that was certain.

"Mind's not changed a bit," he said in an uncompromising, flat tone. "Meant everything I said before— would pleasure me no end to have you for my wife, but I won't tie you down to me. You deserve more than that—tied to a man dodging the law."

"It wouldn't matter to me," Meg said, and once more slipped into a gloomy silence.

They reached the first of the foothills around dark, topped them out onto a short flat, crossed over it, and once again began to climb.

"I reckon we're in Colorado now," Foraker said. "San Luis ought to be over there on the right somewhere. Guess we won't make it today, after all."

The girl remained silent, indicating her disinterest. Foraker, watching closely, wondered if he were making the right decision. It was for her sake, he assured himself; there was nothing he could offer her but hardship and danger; actually, had she been several years older, he still would have been reluctant to let her share the kind of life he was facing—that she was too young only made a union all the more impossible.

He glanced ahead. Off to the left of the trail the were following was one of the old abandoned miner's cabins that dotted the slopes and valleys of the area. Nights in the high mountain country were cold, and since there was no chance of making it to San Luis that day, it would be wise to take shelter in one of the weathered structures.

"We'll put up in there till morning," he said, pointing to the squat log building. "Can build us a fire and maybe keep warm."

Meg only nodded to signify her agreement and began to veer her horse toward the cabin. In the next moment Bart Foraker stiffened in his saddle. A dozen riders broke out of the brush two hundred yards or so to his right. It took but a single glance to recognize Eben Burke and his posse.

"Into the cabin—quick!" he shouted to Meg as a yell went up from the lawmen.

★ 19 ★

Meg did not hesitate. Digging her heels into the sides of her horse, she made a run for the log shack. Gunshots broke out in that same moment, and Foraker, close behind her on the bay, felt the warm brush of a bullet along his face and heard the dull thud of others as they drove into the thick wall of the cabin.

"Around back," he shouted, and as the girl rode her mount to the rear of the aging structure, he followed closely.

There, briefly protected from the fire of the posse, both came off their horses and raced to the partly open door of the cabin. Rushing inside, Foraker shoved the heavy panel shut and dropped the crossbar into its brackets—hearing, as he did, the quick pound of the posse's horses as they closed in.

"The windows—lock the shutters," he yelled to Meg, and hurriedly crossed the room to the front door. It, too, was open slightly, and closing it by putting a shoulder against the thick timber panel, he quickly secured it also.

Wheeling, breathing hard from such hurried activity, he glanced at Meg. She smiled tightly, pointed at the two windows in opposing walls.

"Shut and locked," she said.

Foraker grinned tautly. "Was a close one," he said,

and moved back to the small, circular port near the front door. Crouching slightly, he peered out.

Eben Burke, astride his horse, was sitting in the center of a slowly gathering circle in the failing light. Next to him was Pete Worley. The deputy was talking, gesturing with both hands as he explained or outlined something to the older man. At one time Burke waved him to silence and began himself to talk.

"Looks like we're going to be stuck here for a spell," Foraker said. "I think the sheriff's giving the posse orders to surround the place."

Meg glanced about in the steadily darkening cabin. It was but one room, with a rock fireplace in one wall, bunks for sleeping built against another. In a close-by corner a hole in the roof marked the place where a cook stove once stood, but it and its complementing pipe were now gone, leaving only scorch marks to indicate its previous location.

"They can't get to us in here," Meg said. "Walls are real thick—same as the doors."

Bart smiled, his lips twisting wryly. "Works both ways—no chance of us getting out either."

Meg crossed to one of the bunks and, ignoring the thick accumulation of dust on the slats, sat down. "What can we do? If we—"

"Foraker!" It was Pete Worley's voice. "You hear me?"

Turning back to the front rifle port, Bart answered, "I hear you."

"Want you to come out with your hands up. We've got the place surrounded and every man jack's been told to shoot to kill if you try making a run for it."

Foraker remained silent. It was the end of the road, he reckoned; the cabin had been both a sanctuary and a trap. What mattered now was Meg's safety.

"If'n you don't," Worley continued, "we aim to set fire to the place."

"I've got a young girl in here," Foraker shouted at once. "You try that and I'll put a bullet in every man I can draw a bead on. Got plenty of ports in these walls that'll let me do it!"

There was a pause and then the deputy said, "Seen her riding with you. Where'd you pick her up at?"

"Never you mind about that—just pay heed to what I said."

Again there was a silence, broken this time when Eben Burke spoke up. "I want to give you a chance, Foraker—don't like having to shoot you down. Show some good sense and come out."

Foraker, recognizing the futility of further resistance, but trusting no one insofar as Meg was concerned, said, "I've got this girl to think about, Sheriff. She's got folks in San Luis. You send a man for her uncle—name's Swope—and bring him here. Then we—"

"Hell, I'll take her myself if that's what's bothering you," Pete Worley interrupted. "No use wasting all that time, going and coming. It'd be morning—"

"I'd not trust you with a rattlesnake," Bart cut in coldly. Then, "That's the way it'll have to be, Sheriff. You fetch Swope and we'll talk business."

"It'll be morning before I can send a man," Burke said, mildly protesting.

"All right with me," Foraker replied. "We won't be going nowhere."

Foraker turned, crossed to the back wall, and looked through the rifle port near it. He could see his horse and Meg's grulla grazing unconcernedly on the grass a dozen yards away. There was no sign of any posse member, but there was no doubt in Bart's mind that they were out there completing the ring of guns that encircled the old cabin.

124

"Did you mean that about getting my uncle—or have you got a scheme of some sort in mind?" Meg asked, and before he could answer, she added, "Oh, I wish I had a gun! I'd help you escape from here."

Foraker looked closely at the girl, barely visible now as night, always swift in the high mountain country, closed in.

"Obliged, but I'm not about to let you get mixed up in my troubles."

"I am mixed up in them," Meg declared.

"No, not far as the law's concerned—"

"Maybe so, but that don't mean a thing to me, Bart. I love you, and whatever happens to you I want to happen to me."

"That's fool talk," Foraker exploded. "And you'll listen to me and do what I tell you! Come morning, when your uncle's out there, I'll open the door. You'll walk up to him, then you'll tell him I said to take you and get away from here fast—"

"Then you'll either try to shoot your way out, or you'll just give up—"

He shrugged. "Something I haven't decided yet and you don't need to fret over."

"But if you turn yourself over to that sheriff, you'll get hung for the murder of that woman—"

"Don't forget I didn't do it, and I'm still hoping for a chance to prove it."

"But what if they won't give you that chance—just go ahead soon as they get you, take a rope, and—"

Meg's voice broke. Foraker stepped up to the bunk where she was sitting. Settling down beside her, he put an arm about her.

"Not much chance of that happening—not with Burke along. If it was Pete Worley running things, I could expect to find myself swinging from a tree, but the sheriff will see that I get back to town and stand trial. Anyway, I escaped from them once, just might do it again."

Meg began to sob quietly, and tightening his arm, Foraker held the girl closer. Abruptly, he reached up and, turning her face to his, kissed her firmly on the lips. A small cry escaped Meg, and drawing back, she stared at him through the darkness that filled the cabin.

"Oh, Bart, what—"

"Wanted you to know that you mean everything—the whole world to me, Meg. Saying I wouldn't marry you didn't mean I wasn't in love with you. I guess we feel the same about each other."

Meg's sob renewed, and she buried her face against his chest. "I—I was sure you loved me, but the way you treated me—like you were my brother—I couldn't make myself believe it when you kept pushing me away."

"Was for your own good . . . and still is," Foraker said.

She seemed not to hear. "We can't let it all end here," she murmured. "Why can't we wait until we're sure all those deputies are asleep—they're bound to be as tired as we are—then slip out real quiet and get our horses?"

The words were pouring from the girl's lips, anxious, hopeful, and desperate. "Or maybe I could just go out real quiet like I said, attract the attention of the deputy that's watching the back door. While I keep him busy, you could sneak out, get to the horses, and then I—"

"It wouldn't work," Foraker said, trying to make his words sound as kind as possible.

"But if it did, then we could both start for Mexico, and—"

"Even if it did, I'd not take you with me, Meg," Bart broke in. "Why can't I make you understand?"

"But—but you just said you loved me!"

"I do, and that's why we're going to do things my way. In the morning I'll wait until I see you ride off with your uncle, then I'll make a deal with Burke, tell him I'll hand myself over to him if he'll see to it that I get a fair trial. He's honest, I figure, and I can depend on his word."

Meg listened quietly until he had finished, and then shook her head. "I'm afraid it will mean the end for us."

"Maybe, but the way I see it we don't have much choice. Like I've said, I got away from them once, and if things don't go right for me at the trial, there's a good chance I can get away again. Thing for you to do is go along with your uncle and wait."

"Wait?"

"Yes, I'll light out for Mexico once I'm loose—and I'll get there this time."

"How long will I have to wait?"

"Probably take a couple of years, but you can figure on me coming back; and if you still feel the same about me then as you do now—you'll be seventeen by that time—we can marry up. Meantime, while you're being patient, you can be making things for your hope chest and getting it filled up. Too, you can sort of look around, meet some other fellows, be sure I'm the one you want to spend the rest of your life with, because with me marriage is a forever thing."

"I'll not change my mind—never. But two years—why will it take such a long time?"

"Things will have to simmer down up here, and while I'm waiting, I'll be trying to get something put together for us—a life of some kind.

"There's a rancher over Texas way that I worked for once who told me if I ever wanted a job again to come back. Said he'd make me his foreman. The pay would be good, and there's a little house, I recollect, that goes with the job. But I can't go to him, ask him to hire me

127

until my name's clear. Just wouldn't be right, me sign-
ing up with a price on my head."

Meg stirred. "But that's all if you escape. What if you
can't?"

He smiled at her in the darkness. "We won't be thinking about that. Can't see no other answer, anyway.
Burke's got too many deputies strung around us. We'd
not get twenty feet if we tried making a break for the
horses."

"I guess you're right," Meg said after a bit. "And
maybe I could help when you go to stand trial. I could
ask my uncle to go with me, and maybe we could find—"

A quick tapping sounded on the back door of the
cabin. Foraker and the girl came off the bunk together
as he raised his hand for silence. Moving quietly, they
crossed to the rear of the cabin.

Again the sound came, short but insistent. Foraker
pressed up close to the wall and peered through the rifle
port. In the pale light he could make out a vague shape
hunkered at the door. And then a hoarse whisper
reached him.

"Damn it, Foraker, let me in! It's me, Reno!"

Reno!

Anger rose in Foraker. Crockett had a lot of guts to be showing up after the way he'd thrown in with Gilley and those other outlaws!

"What do you want?"

"In, that's what," Crockett replied in the same hoarse, urgent way. "Got a scheme that'll get you out of the hole you've put yourself in."

Foraker gave that thought. He didn't trust Reno Crockett at all, not after the double-cross he'd pulled, and for the outlaw to have made a deal with Eben Burke to save his own neck would come as no surprise. Crowding up close to the wall, Bart looked out, probing the darkness around the outlaw carefully. He could see no one, no dim figures waiting to rush the door once opened, reckoned that Crockett actually was alone. Lifting the bar, Foraker drew back the heavy panel a narrow distance. Reno was through and inside within an instant.

"Damn it all," the outlaw muttered, halting in the center of the room. "Was starting to think you was going to leave me out there, let one of them tin stars spot me!"

Bart had shut the door and replaced the bar. "No big reason why I should turn a hand for you—not after that

129

.t you pulled the other night when Gilley and your
er friends showed up."

"Was a damn-fool thing to do," Reno admitted, "but
I figured I'd best line up with Ben because my chances
would be better. Hell, I just played my hand wrong—
ain't you ever gone and made a mistake? . . . Howdy,
missy, you all right?" he added, glancing at Meg, again
sitting on the edge of the bunk.

The girl nodded coolly, arms folded, while she
watched narrowly.

"You still heading back for Mexico when you get the
little lady delivered in San Luis?" Reno asked, turning
to Foraker.

"What I'm figuring, if—"

"If you get out of this here pocket you've got yourself
in," Reno finished. "That's what brought me up here—
going to Mexico with you. I split with Ben Gilley and
them other boys when we got to Vegas. They wanted to
hang around for a spell, but I was scared I'd run into
some damned lawman with my name in his pocket.

"Stayed clear of the place after me and them'd had a
couple of drinks in a saloon at the edge of town—and
just kept riding north, hoping I'd spot you and the little
gal. You sure must've hung close to them hills, because I
never seen you till this morning."

"You didn't know that Gilley and the others threw in
with a posse at Las Vegas and was looking for me—you,
too, maybe?"

"Nope, sure didn't. You have a run-in with them?"

"Up on the side of the mountain. Winged the Texan
and some other jasper, and put Gilley down for good,
shooting my way out of it."

"Whoo—eee! Must've been a whole bucket of fun! I
guess old Ben was trying to put himself in good with the
law by joining up with a posse."

"Wasn't the law. They've tacked a thousand-dollar reward on each of us—dead or alive. That bunch he and his friends lined up with were just some barflies and cowhands looking to pick up some easy money."

Crockett whistled. "A thousand dollars, eh? Good thing I ditched Ben when I did, or they'd been plugging me and doing some collecting."

Meg came off the bunk and, crossing the room, took up a stand beside Foraker. "You got by the deputies and got in here—do you think you can get us out?"

"Done said I come here so's Foraker and me can go to Mexico. He's my ticket."

"If you're thinking we can shoot our way out, you're fooling yourself," Bart said. "Burke's got a ring of deputies around this place that'll be hard to get past—which has set me to wondering . . . how'd you get by them?"

"Wasn't hard," Reno said expansively. "When I spotted you this morning, you was west of me. I'd misfigured where you'd likely be—never was no good at geography and things like that. Started across to catch you, and just about did when Burke and his damned posse showed up right in between you and me, so I real quick dropped back out of sight.

"I seen you make a run for this here cabin, heard that son-of-a-bitching Worley talking to you, and after him, the sheriff. Couldn't hear what you was saying to them, but when I seen Burke string out his deputies, I figured you'd told them to plumb go straight to hell.

"Well, I waited out till things had sort of settled down, then I circled the cabin and come up from behind it till I spotted the back door. Better'n the front because there's more cover. Was no big deal then to locate the deputy that was watching the back of the place, slip up Indianlike on him, and put him out of business."

Foraker had listened in silence to Crockett's explanation of how he had gotten to the cabin. It sounded logical, but he was still suspicious of the outlaw and was refusing to accept everything Reno had said at face value. Crockett would sell him out in an instant—and without batting an eye, he was certain—yet Eben Burke didn't seem to be the sort of lawman who'd bargain with an outlaw, epecially one of Reno Crockett's like, under any circumstances.

But there was no denying the fact he was in a desperate tight, and if there was a chance that he and Meg could escape, he should take it. Crockett got past the deputies that surrounded the cabin—it could follow that he and Meg could also slip by them.

"If you've got a scheme for getting us out of here, let's hear it," he said. "But if it will put Meg in any kind of danger, you can forget it. I'll go ahead with what I—"

"Hell," Crockett said in disgust. "Anything we try's going to be risky, and since she's in here and a part of it, she'll have to take her chances, same as we will.

"Just going to have to make a choice—either you're willing to try or you ain't. Far as I'm concerned I'm getting back out of here—same way I come in. I sure ain't figuring to just set around, wait for them to come after me."

Foraker felt Meg's fingers upon his arm. "Don't worry about me—I'll be all right as long as I'm with you."

"That's the way to talk, little lady," Reno said enthusiastically. "I figured all along you was a fighter!"

Foraker shrugged. Reno Crockett wasn't fooling him; Reno was thinking of himself, not of Meg; he was willing to do, or say, anything that would enable him to get safely to Mexico.

"Let's hear your plan," he said.

"Ain't nothing much to it," Crockett said, lowering his voice. "I want you and the gal to get out of here, same way I come in, while it's still dark. It's kind of cloudy out, so if you keep down low, ain't nobody going to spot you."

"What about the horses? They still out there?"

"Over there to the right, grazing. Mine's with them, and so's that deputy's I put under. You get to them it'll be best you lead them off a ways real quietlike, then mount up and head for this here San Luis."

"What'll you be doing?"

"Setting right here making noise now and then so's Burke and them others'll figure you're still around. I'll give you a couple of hours, then I'll slip out, get my horse, and meet you down the trail. You recollect that big pine that'd been hit by lightning and was laying across the trail?"

Foraker nodded. "About two miles back—"

"That's it. When you hand over the little gal to her kinfolk, swing wide of here and meet me there. I'll be waiting. Then we can light out for Mexico and be a far piece from here before Burke and them badge-toters even know we're gone. That sound jake to you?"

Again Foraker was aware of Meg's fingers gently pressing into his arm. He laid his hand upon hers reassuringly.

"Ought to work," he admitted, and turning to a nearby rifle port, looked out into the night.

Although the moon and starlight were both weak, thanks to a cloud-streaked sky, they should by using care be able to leave the cabin without being seen. By removing the deputy placed directly opposite the door of the shack, Reno had eliminated the man who would have made an escape impossible; now, with no one there watching, it should be a fairly simple task.

"Want you and the gal to move out right away," Reno said, taking charge. "I'll give you a few minutes, then start a racket just in case somebody out there gets suspicious."

Foraker signified his understanding. Then, "How long do you aim to wait before you move out?"

"Ain't sure—how far is it to this here San Luis?"

"Probably ten miles—"

"Then I'll hang around a couple of hours, like I already said. You've got to have time enough to circle back and be at that old pine when I get there."

"Best you don't push your luck," Foraker warned. "Might be smarter if you stalled around for only an hour—"

Crockett laughed. "Now, don't go trying to tell grandpa how to shuck corn! This here's my idea, and I've got it all figured out. You just do like I say and everything will work out fine. . . . You ready?"

Foraker looked down at Meg. Although she was at his side, her features were barely distinguishable in the weak light filtering into the cabin through the rifle ports and the stovepipe hole in the roof.

"Reckon so," Bart said, and taking the girl by the hand, started for the door.

Reno moved quickly ahead of them, and quietly lifting the crossbar, opened the panel a few inches and looked out.

"Just like it was," he said in a low, satisfied voice. "Can see your horses off there to the right—same place as before. Now, hunch down low and don't stop to pick no pretty daisies once you're out of here."

Meg and Foraker dropped to a crouch. Reno opened the door a bit wider to allow their exit.

"Good luck, pardner," he whispered as they moved by him.

Bart Foraker murmured a response, and holding Meg's hand, eased out into the night.

★ 21 ★

Foraker, once outside the cabin, quickly drew Meg into the shadows lying off to one side. There in the darkness he glanced about, making certain that there were no deputies waiting, that Reno Crockett hadn't tricked him. All was quiet, and locating the horses, he led the girl hurriedly across the narrow strip of open ground into the deep cover of the brush beyond and then to where the horses waited.

Working quietly, Bart approached the animals from the front, being doubly careful not to frighten them into setting up a noise or, worse, causing them to race off into the trees.

But his fears were unnecessary; Reno had taken time to secure the reins of their two mounts to a convenient juniper, but had tethered his as well as that of the deputy he had taken care of, thus eliminating the possibility of the animals setting up a disturbance or running away.

"We'll lead them a piece," Bart whispered to Meg, handing her the leathers to her mount.

Stepping out ahead, reins in one hand, pistol in the other, Foraker chose a course that took them on a straight line from the cabin. There would be deputies stationed at various points around the old structure, and the only way to avoid those nearby was to get as far as possible from them before swinging eastward for San Luis.

Over in front of the cabin they could see the glare of the lawmen's fire, built, no doubt, so that it showed plainly the door of the cabin. Why they had not followed a like procedure at the rear, Foraker could not understand; likely Burke expected him to leave the shack by the front, where he had set up camp, and didn't feel it necessary to do more than maintain a token watch on the rear.

Certainly the men assigned the task of watching the back door from the brush nearby would see anyone emerging, but the lawman had not taken into consideration, apparently, what the situation would be should the key man—the guard directly opposite the door—was removed.

Bart took no chances. He led Meg and the horses for a good two hundred yards due west through the fairly heavy undergrowth and then, mounting up, began a wide circle toward the east.

They drew abreast the cabin, easily located through the flare of yellow firelight, a time later as they doubled back for the settlement. They could not see any of the posse, due to the brush and trees, but they could hear voices and guessed that some of the deputies were gathered about the fire dispelling the chill that, at such high altitude, had begun to settle in shortly after dark. A disturbing thought came to Foraker as they moved, now at a faster pace, through the night.

"Sure hope they're not taking turns at warming themselves. If they are, they're going to come across that deputy Reno killed."

Meg said, "They won't have any idea who did it, and far as they'll know, we'll still be inside the cabin."

He nodded. "You're right, but it could make it harder for Reno to get away when he makes his move. The whole posse could start beating the brush looking for whoever did it."

"I see," the girl murmured.

They rode on, holding to as good a pace as possi through the heavy growth and plentiful trees th studded the hills. Foraker was anxious to get Meg safely into the hands of her relatives—not that he'd be particularly glad to see the last of her, but because he wanted to be at the appointed place and time to meet Reno. Too, if the outlaw had trouble getting past the deputies, it was only right that he go to the man's aid.

Bart raised himself in the stirrups and looked ahead. They should be seeing signs of the town, he felt. He had spotted Purgatory Peak off to their right and straight on a distance; the settlement, he thought, was not too far from it. Meg, of course, never having been there before, had no idea at all where San Luis lay.

And then a half-hour or so later a light broke the vast darkness before them. A hard grin cracked Foraker's lips, erasing the disturbing thought that he might have bypassed the town in the darkness. San Luis was just ahead, and urging the horses to a lope, they hurried toward the lonely beacon in the night.

The light proved to be coming from a window of the town's only saloon doing business at that hour. Pulling up before it, Bart and Meg glanced about at the sparse scatter of houses barely visible to them.

"It'll save time to ask where your uncle's place is," he said, and dismounting, entered the small building.

Only two patrons were in evidence, both wearing miner's garb, and neither looked up as he crossed to the bar, a rough, plank affair placed across a pair of sawhorses.

"Looking for the Swopes. Can you tell me how to get there?" he said when the bartender, a man in a thick red shirt and faded overalls, faced him.

The saloon keeper nodded, his lumpy features expressionless. "Expect I can. Take the road on east—

137

's the one running alongside my place—and Tom ope's the second farm on the right."

"Obliged to you," Foraker said, and started to turn away.

"Seems a man traveling late like you are and asking questions ought to be good for a drink," the bartender said grumpily.

Foraker paused, reached into a pocket, and drew out a half-dollar. Dropping it on the counter, he said, "You're right, mister—but I'm a mite short of time right now, so you treat yourself," and hurried on out the door.

Swinging up into the saddle, Bart repeated the directions given him in the saloon as they pulled away from the hitch rack.

"That won't be far," Meg said in a dull voice. "I guess we ought to say our good-byes now. I know you have to get back to Reno."

Foraker nodded. "I keep thinking about the chance he took to get us out of that cabin, and the one he'll be taking when he leaves. Want to be there if he runs into trouble. Sure, I know he did it as much for himself as he did for us, but way I see it, that don't change anything."

"I understand," Meg said. "When you see him again, tell him I'm grateful, too, for what he did."

"I'll do that. . . . Guess that's your uncle's place there ahead—on the right," Foraker said, pointing to a cluster of peaked- and slanted-roof buildings. "Looks like a mighty fine farm."

"I guess it is," Meg said lifelessly. "I was hoping you would stay, meet my uncle and his family—and maybe we could talk—"

"Nothing I'd like better, but you know what I'm up against," Foraker said, drawing the bay in close to the girl's horse as they halted at the gate. Leaning over, he took Meg in his arms and kissed her.

138

"Can look for me two years from now—might even be sooner. Anyway, I'll write when I sort of get settled."

The girl clung to him, returned his kisses with her own. "Two years—that's so long, so far off. Bart, I don't want you to go! I'm afraid we'll never see each other again."

"Don't believe that—not for a minute," Foraker said gently. "I'm not about to lose you. Two years is a long time for me, too, but when I look at you, I know it'll be worth it, Now, *adiós*, as they say down New Mexico way, *vaya con Dios*."

Meg drew back from him, shook her head. "I don't know what that means, but I love you—and please come back."

"Can bet on that," Foraker replied, cutting the bay around. "You'll have a mighty hard time getting rid of me—"

A distant crackle of gunshots echoed faintly through the cool night's hush. Bart drew up stiffly in his saddle. Another spatter of reports sounded.

"Reno!" Foraker muttered aloud. "He's in trouble!"

Raking the gelding with his spurs, Bart sent the big horse rushing ahead through the darkness.

Crockett held the cabin door ajar a narrow crack and watched Foraker and the girl slip off into the shadows. When he could no longer see them, he quickly closed the panel and dropped the crossbar into its brackets. They had made it to the horses, they should have no difficulty from there on.

Turning, he crossed to the rifle port in the front of the cabin, put an eye to it, and looked out. Three men were tossing brush into a pile preparatory to building a fire. One he recognized as Pete Worley, the others he reckoned he might have seen back in Red Bluff, but he wasn't sure—not that it mattered a damn.

139

He located Sheriff Eben Burke when the flames lifted and threw a circle of light in the area fronting the cabin. The lawman was hunched, back to a tree, a short distance off to one side. Reno grinned; old Eben would be mad enough to spit fire when he found out he'd lost his prisoner again! Good thing he'd never know that both of them he'd had in charge, and let escape, were right there under his nose.

"Old bastard'd throw a fit," Crockett said, turning away.

Crossing to the bunk, he sat down and leaned back, wishing, as he did, that he had something to drink or smoke, but he was without both. When he was with Ben Gilley and the two jaspers riding with him—Hobie Green and John Willie Poe—he'd mooched the makings for a few cigarettes with the promise that when they got to Vegas he'd lay in a supply of both tobacco and liquor.

He couldn't make good on that, of course, since he was flat broke, but he never let Ben and the others know it. And when they'd got to Vegas, he'd ridden on, wanting not only to avoid all possibilities of running into the law, but also to join up with Foraker again so that he could ride with him to Mexico.

Mexico . . . he'd heard a man could do real good down there. Americans, he'd been told, could always find jobs in the mines as foremen, or in the saloons—*cantinas*, they called them—running the games. He'd been a pretty fair hand at gambling a few years back—before he'd given it all up and started drifting. He reckoned he could be so again, once he had done a bit of practicing.

He should've stayed in Wichita, Reno reminded himself now just as he had a hundred times in the past, hung on to that job he had in a Douglas Street saloon in Wichita. He'd done right well there, had himself a fat stake put aside, and was thinking about opening up a place of his own.

Then he'd met Alicia. She blew into town from New Orleans—hair black as night with eyes to match; skin like alabaster but soft as a desert primrose; generous hips, a full bosom, and a wide sparkling smile. He'd gone for her straight off—rope, spurs, saddle, and all.

They had started hitting the high spots shortly after they had met—Abilene, Hays, Dodge City, and all intermediate points, Wichita included—and kept at it for a solid month. And then one morning he had awakened to find himself alone in bed. Alicia was gone. So was his stake, and all he had to show for both were memories of good times.

He'd begun to drift after that, going from town to town, gambling a little, working cattle when he was forced to, even doing a stint as a deputy sheriff up in Montana. From there he'd wandered down into Colorado, halting finally in a town called Trinidad. He killed a man there in an argument over cards, and thereby got the law on his trail.

They nailed him a short time later, threw him in what served as a jail in the town of Red Bluff, up close to the Kansas border, in Nebraska—and that's where he tied in with Bart Foraker.

Foraker . . . Reno reckoned it was time he stirred up a bit of noise, let the law outside know there was somebody, presumably Foraker and his girlfriend, inside the cabin. Rising, he stepped away from the bunk, moved to the front door, and lifting the crossbar, rattled it vigorously. Peering through the rifle port he saw several of the deputies glance toward the cabin. One made a remark of some sort, whereupon they all laughed.

That done, Crockett returned to the bunk and sat down again, wishing once more he had a drink of

141

whiskey or something to smoke. But as before, he brushed off the desire simply because there was nothing available, and put his mind on what lay ahead.

He'd stall an hour longer before he headed for the rendezvous. That would give Foraker plenty of time to get shed of the girl and head back for the meeting place. It was still several hours until first light when Eben Burke would be expecting Foraker to turn himself in— or try to escape—so there was really no big rush. But to be on the safe side, he'd not wait too long.

Sitting there in the dark, Reno caught himself dozing, and at once got to his feet and began to pace back and forth. Falling asleep at this stage of the game was the last thing he wanted to happen; he just might go past the safe time to leave—and that would put him right in the hands of Burke and the posse while Bart Foraker would be getting away safely.

Crockett continued to move about the cabin, only now and then pausing to sit on the bunk for a few minutes' rest. Then, finally restlessness overcame him; he could remain in the shack no longer and, crossing to the back door, carefully let himself out.

There was no sign of deputies anywhere, and when he reached his horse, the gray standing beside him was still there, which told Reno that the deputy he'd sent under had not been found. Leading his horse off for a short distance, Crockett mounted and cut left, pointing direct for the trail south and the lightning-shattered pine where he was to meet Bart Foraker.

Abruptly a rider appeared before Reno—coming out of the dense, darkness-filled brush. The deputy uttered a startled oath, yelled, and grabbed for his gun. Crockett shot him through the heart before he could get his weapon out of leather.

"Damn it to hell!" he swore, spurring his horse and sending him plunging ahead into the night. The shot

would bring other lawmen; they would think F[c]
was making a break to escape. The big surprise w[e]
be when they found out it was him, not Foraker, a[.]
that Bart was already gone.

"Over here," a voice shouted from his right. "Over
here!"

Another deputy, one on foot, ran into the open, his
rifle raised. Reno fired twice, the shots so close as to almost be together. Both smashed into the man, knocked
him back into the brush.

"It's Crockett!"

The cry came from his left this time. Immediately a
rider bolted into view, blocking his way. Pete Worley! A
hard grin cracked Reno's mouth. He owed Worley a
couple of lumps.

"Have a good time in hell, Worley," he shouted, and
triggered his weapon.

Worley fired in that same fragment of time. Reno
rocked back in his saddle as a slug tore into his chest.
He grabbed the horn, hung on, seeing Pete Worley fall
from his horse. The hard grin now a grimace of con-
tempt, Crockett dug spurs into his mount and rushed
on.

★ 22 ★

Foraker, forsaking the plan of circling wide to avoid the cabin and coming onto the trail well below it, headed for the old structure on a direct line. Something had gone wrong, he felt certain, and if so, Reno could be in need of help.

Crouched low over the saddle, Bart held the bay to a good lope. The sky to the east was now slowly brightening with the first hint of daylight, and it was becoming easier to see, which made it possible to cut across brushy land without regard to the trail or wagon road.

He heard more shots and spurred the gelding to a faster gallop, but when he topped out a short hill a bit later and saw the cabin a quarter-mile or so away, he slowed the animal to a trot. Then, holding the bay to that gait, Bart rode down the rise and began to carefully circle the old structure.

He had no idea what to expect, could in no way tell if Crockett was still within the cabin or somewhere outside in the steadily lightening woods. His guess was that Reno had made it into the open, was heading for the rendezvous at the burned pine, and had encountered one or several of the deputies.

The question answered itself a short time later as he was walking his horse quietly, a hundred yards or so west of the cabin, through the heavy brush.

144

"You see him?" a voice farther along in the g. yelled.

"Nope, sure don't—but he can't've got far. Was i bad."

"Heard Pete say he was heading back down the trail when he plugged him."

"How is Worley?"

"Plenty bad hurt. Damned outlaw got him dead center."

Foraker pulled the bay to a halt, considered what he had just heard. Reno, according to what had been said, was in a bad way. Evidently the outlaw and Pete Worley had run into each other and shot it out, with the result that both were badly wounded. And since Crockett had been on his way for the meeting at the blackened pine, it was logical that he'd now be somewhere along the trail.

Keeping in the shadow-filled brush as much as possible, Foraker struck a course closely paralleling the path. Twice he was forced to stop and draw back into the thick growth when he heard a rider passing nearby. Eben Burke apparently had every man in the posse searching for Reno Crockett; the lawman would be aware by then, also, that he had slipped through the ring of deputies encircling the cabin and would be intensifying the hunt for Reno in hopes of prying information from the outlaw as to where his partner would be.

"Foraker—"

Bart heard his name called. The voice was low, cautious, or possibly very weak. He drew to a halt, glanced about.

"Here—"

Foraker veered to his left. No more than a half-dozen strides from the trail he saw Reno Crockett. The outlaw was lying in a shallow wash, had pulled dead leaves and branches over himself to conceal his presence. Bart

145

d around, listened. He could hear no one. Coming
the saddle, he hurried to the man and crouched
side him.

"You bad hit?"

"Reckon so. Figured you was one of them deputies
that's scouting for me. Was all set to blow your damn
head off."

Foraker drew himself upright. He could now hear a
rider somewhere over to the left, but from the diminish-
ing sound he guessed the man was going away from
them. In the direction of the cabin voices were shouting
back and forth, but he was unable to make out the
words. Again he knelt beside Crockett.

"Light's getting stronger—we've got to get out of here.
Think you can ride?"

"Ride what? Damned horse of mine spooked and run
the hell away. I—"

"I'll put you on mine," Bart cut in, and started to
help the outlaw rise.

"Be wasting your time, pard," Reno said. "I'm going
under for sure. . . . You ain't said—did you find the
little gal's folks?"

"Yes, was no trouble."

"You aiming to marry up with her?"

"No, too young, besides it'd be the wrong thing to do
with the law on my back. If I can get straight, I'll come
back in a couple of years. . . . Now, button up your
lip and put your arm around my neck so's I can get you
on your feet."

"Expect I've got a better idea," Crockett said. "You
light out and I'll stay right here, keep any of them
badge-toters from following—"

"The hell with your idea," Foraker snapped. "Come
on, help me get you up. My horse is close by."

Reno managed to pull himself to a sitting position,
and then, with Foraker's support, got to his feet.

146

"Wasting your time," he muttered.

Bart ignored the protest and half-carried, half-walked the outlaw the short distance to where the bay stood. Getting Reno into the saddle was a matter of sheer strength, but he managed it. Then, breathing hard, Bart spent several moments listening to see if the activity had attracted any attention. He could hear no one and took up the gelding's reins.

"Hang on to the horn," he told the outlaw, keeping his voice low. "Soon as we get clear of here, I'll get up behind you."

"Sure, sure," Reno muttered, clutching the saddle horn with both hands as he sagged forward. In the growing light his sandy, bewhiskered features were a chalk color and his small, sharp eyes appeared to have receded into his head. Blood soaked the front of his shirt and the bandanna he had crammed into the bullet wound in his chest.

"I put a couple of slugs in that damn Worley," he mumbled. "Sure hope it didn't do him any good."

"Heard a couple of the deputies talking about it when I was coming up," Foraker replied quietly as they moved off through the heavy growth. "Sounded like they didn't figure he'd make it."

"That pleasures me a lot," the outlaw said in a satisfied tone. "The son of a bitch had it coming to him."

Bart glanced about, fearful of encountering one of the searching deputies. "Best we don't talk—leastwise not until we get a fair piece from here," he cautioned. "Not sure just where—"

"Here—over here! Here's both of them," a man sang out suddenly from the brush nearby.

Instantly Foraker dropped the leathers he was holding and, whipping out his gun, snapped a shot at the deputy.

The lawman yelled as the bullet, fired hastily, grazed

147

his cheek. He dragged out his own weapon, tried to throw down on Foraker, but his horse was shying wildly. Bart triggered a second bullet. The man flinched as the slug caught him in the upper part of the leg. Other riders, attracted by the deputy's yell and the gunshots, were closing in. Foraker pivoted to Crockett.

"Hang on! I'll catch up with you," he said in a hoarse whisper, and forcing the reins into the outlaw's hands locked to the saddle horn, slapped the bay gelding sharply on the hindquarters and sent him loping off into the trees.

Turning back around, Bart faced the riders coming up from the direction of the cabin. There were three of them, all closely bunched as they sought to avoid the hindering brush by staying on the trail.

Foraker threw a quick shot over their heads, and as they instantly separated and swerved off into the thick growth, he ducked back in behind a stand of junipers, reloading his forty-five—actually Pete Worley's gun, he recalled in that moment—as he ran. Yells were lifting behind him, blending with the dust and powder smoke, and he knew that in only moments the lawmen would have recovered themselves and come charging at him with weapons blazing.

Pistol cylinder full, Foraker cut sharply to his right, started doubling back toward the cabin. He wanted in no way to lead the deputies into the direction he'd sent Reno, but he shouldn't get too far from the wounded outlaw.

A rider abruptly raced across a small clearing directly in front of him. The deputy saw Foraker first, triggered the rifle he was holding, from the hip. The bullet was wide, but Foraker's was not; the man, clawing at his shoulder, rocked to one side, lost his stirrups, and fell to the ground.

"Over this way!"

148

The deputy's shout was unnecessary as the gunshots gave away Foraker's position. At once he altered direction and, sucking hard for wind, plunged off into the brush and trees. Daylight was now complete, and he no longer had the protection of the deep shadows, could rely only on the thick growth and the tree trunks for cover.

He cut sharp left, ran hard for a dozen yards, and then reversing himself, began to double back. Riders were seemingly all around him now, and it was difficult to decide which way was the best to turn. A riderless horse loomed up straight ahead. Bart slowed his headlong flight and carefully eased up to the animal.

A chunky, powerful-looking buckskin, the horse stood quiet until Foraker got him and grabbed the reins. At that moment the buckskin started to shy off, jerking wildly at the leathers, but Bart had a firm grip on the reins and the cantle of the saddle and literally vaulted onto the nervous animal.

He wasn't certain if he was any better off than he had been. On foot it was possible to dodge in and out among the trees and brush and take advantage of the weed clumps; on a horse, however, he probably would be less noticeable among the deputies, who were all mounted; too, he could move faster.

Keeping the buckskin pointed straight ahead—away from the confusion of riders, whipping back and forth, shouting questions, yelling, and cursing, Foraker began to breathe a bit easier. It had been nip and tuck there for a few minutes, but now it appeared he'd managed somehow to break out of the encirclement of lawmen Eben Burke had thrown around the area below the cabin. If luck continued to run with him, he'd soon be well beyond them, could then turn left and look for Reno Crockett.

It didn't take long. Foraker, after angling more to the

149

south, shortly spotted his bay horse standing patiently in a grassy swale, grazing indifferently. The saddle was empty.

Urging the buckskin to a trot, Bart reached the big gelding. Nearby Reno lay where he had fallen—half in a narrow wash. Dismounting hurriedly, Foraker crossed to the outlaw and, taking him by the arms, pulled him about to where he was in a more comfortable position. Crockett looked up at Bart, a frown on his blanched features.

"Where—where the hell did you come from?"

"Been dodging Burke and his deputies. Thick as flies out there—"

"Seen a couple. . . . The little gal—she all right?"

Reno's mind had slipped. He had already asked about Meg Swope.

"She's fine—said for me to thank you for helping us get out of that cabin. We'll be marrying in a couple of years."

"That's fine, real fine," Crockett said. "Sure hope you and her can make it. I ain't had much use for women since Alicia—"

"Alicia? Who's Alicia?"

Crockett stirred, "Don't matter . . . sure could use a shot of whiskey."

"Wish I had a bottle for you," Foraker said. "Can soon get some. There's a saloon over in San Luis. Can go there if you can ride."

Foraker knew it was a pointless idea. Reno's eyes closed, opened slowly with much effort. A half-smile pulled at his bloodless lips.

"Just don't think I can," he said, and going slack, he turned his head to one side and was dead.

Foraker remained hunched by the outlaw for a long minute, and then, conscious of his precarious situation, rose and crossed quickly to the buckskin he was riding.

A blanket roll was on the saddle, and freeing the square of wool, Bart returned to where the outlaw lay, wrapped it about the man's limp shape, and placed him in the wash. Then, caving in the sides, he finished off the grave by piling stones upon it as he and Crockett had done when they buried the members of the Swope wagon train.

Finished, Bart stepped back. He hadn't particularly liked Reno, had become a partner only through circumstances, but he was a man, and every man deserved a decent burial . . .

"That Crockett?"

★ 23 ★

At the sound of Eben Burke's voice Foraker wheeled and reached for his gun. A heaviness settled through him as he let the weapon slide back into its holster. While he had been seeing to Reno Crockett's burial, the lawman, with a half a dozen deputies, had quietly moved in on him. He nodded to the sheriff. There was no point in denial—no point to anything now.

"Got a few of my own men to bury, thanks to him—and you," Burke said, "but I reckon dying and burying goes with the job."

"It's a hard life," Foraker said dryly.

"One of them we'll be planting is Pete Worley. Your partner there cashed him in."

Foraker started to correct the statement, explain that Reno Crockett was not his partner in the usual sense of the word, but he shrugged and let it pass. It made no difference now.

"What I'm getting around to saying is that Pete Worley done some talking when he was dying. Confessed it was him that killed that rancher's wife, not you."

Foraker felt a tremendous weight lift from his shoulders and a brightness flood into his mind.

"Means you're free to go your way," Burke continued, brushing at his jaw. There was a dullness to the old lawman's eyes and the sagging lines in his face bespoke the weariness the search had laid upon him.

152

"I'm mighty sorry if I made things a bit hard on you, but Pete had me fooled same as he had all the rest of us. There anything I can do to make things right?"

Bart shook his head. There was nothing anybody could do to erase all the hell and tension and strain he'd gone through since Burke and his posse had picked him up that day and brought him in to face a murder charge. The only answer was to try and forget it.

"Obliged, but there's nothing, Sheriff," he said coldly, and turning to the bay, swung into the saddle. Jerking a thumb at the buckskin he'd been riding, he said, "Horse belongs to one of your men. I was just borrowing him," he added, and rode off toward the trail.

Reaching the path, Bart came to a halt; only then did it dawn on him that he no longer needed to seek safety in Mexico. He could come and go again as he pleased, just as he had in the past.

A troubled frown creased his brow. He was at a crossroads. He could continue on, as if going to Mexico, but instead cut over to Texas and look up the rancher who'd offered him a job. He would not be faced now with staying beyond the border and hoping one day to clear himself of a murder charge, but could start right then to make plans for the future—for a life with Meg Swope, to begin—when she was seventeen—two years from then.

Was it really necessary to wait two whole years now that Pete Worley's confession had cleared him in the eyes of the law?

The deputy had solved only half of the problem; Meg was still too young to become a wife—that hadn't changed; and he wouldn't let it, even though he felt a keen desire to have her with him.

He reckoned he should ride on—not go back to San Luis and tell her that he no longer was wanted by the law, that he was going on to Texas to see if a job still awaited him there.

Bart knew immediately what the girl's reaction would be. She would press him to take her along, now that the major obstacle to their future—in her estimation—had been removed. He would have to stand firm, try to make her understand that she must wait, grow up two more years' worth—that she should be certain that a life with him was what she wanted and not just a girlish fancy.

Foraker, brushing nervously at the sweat on his face, gave the matter deep thought. It would be a tearful, heartrending experience, one he would hate to put Meg through. He supposed he could let matters stand just as they did when they said good-bye a few hours earlier. By so doing he could spare her, and himself, the wrenching moments that would come if he was to lay the truth before her. But not to tell her would be the same as a lie—and he'd not start his life with Meg based on one.

Sighing, Bart Foraker cut his horse about and started for San Luis.

Ray Hogan is an author who has inspired a loyal following over the years since he published his first Western novel *Ex-marshal* in 1956. Hogan was born in Willow Springs, Missouri, where his father was town marshal. At five the Hogan family moved to Albuquerque where Ray Hogan still lives in the foothills of the Sandia and Manzano mountains. His father was on the Albuquerque police force and, in later years, owned the Overland Hotel. It was while listening to his father and other old-timers tell tales from the past that Ray was inspired to recast these tales in fiction. From the beginning he did exhaustive research into the history and the people of the Old West and the walls of his study are lined with various firearms, spurs, pictures, books, and memorabilia, about all of which he can talk in dramatic detail. Among his most popular works are the series of books about Shawn Starbuck, a searcher in a quest for a lost brother, who has a clear sense of right and wrong and who is willing to stand up and be counted when it is a question of fairness or justice. His other major series is about lawman John Rye whose reputation has earned him the sobriquet The Doomsday Marshal. 'I've attempted to capture the courage and bravery of those men and women that lived out West and the dangers and problems they had to overcome,' Hogan once remarked. If his lawmen protagonists seem sometimes larger than life, it is because they are men of integrity, heroes who through grit of character and common sense are able to overcome the obstacles they encounter despite often overwhelming odds. This same grit of character can also be found in Hogan's heroines and, in *The Vengeance of Fortuna West*, Hogan wrote a gripping and totally believable account of a woman who takes up the badge and tracks the men who killed her lawman husband by ambush. No less intriguing in her way is Nellie Dupray, convicted of rustling in *The Glory Trail*. Above all, what is most impressive about Hogan's Western novels is the consistent quality with which each is crafted, the compelling depth of his characters, and his ability to juxtapose the complexities of human conflict into narratives always as intensely interesting as they are emotionally involving. His latest novel is *Soldier in Buckskin*.